Creative Writing From Southern Scotland

Edited by Heather Killingray

First published in Great Britain in 2001 by
YOUNG WRITERS
Remus House,
Coltsfoot Drive,
Peterborough, PE2 9JX
Telephone (01733) 890066

HB ISBN 0 75432 700 0
SB ISBN 0 75432 701 9

FOREWORD

This year Young Writers proudly presents a showcase of the best 'Days Of Our Lives . . .' short stories, from up-and-coming writers nationwide.

To write a short story is a difficult exercise. We made it more challenging by setting the theme of 'A Day In The Life Of Someone From The Second Millennium', using no more than 250 words! Much imagination and skill is required. *Days Of Our Lives . . . Creative Writing From Southern Scotland* achieves and exceeds these requirements. This exciting anthology will not disappoint the reader.

The thought, effort, imagination and hard work put into each story impressed us all, and again, the task of editing proved demanding due to the quality of entries received, but was nevertheless enjoyable.

We hope you are as pleased as we are with the final selection and that you continue to enjoy *Days Of Our Lives . . . Creative Writing From Southern Scotland* for many years to come.

CONTENTS

Stenhousemuir Primary School

Nicola McKenzie	194
Caitlin Robb	195
Robbie Blair	196
Darryl Extance	197
Nicole Innes	198
Caitlin Heggie	199
Emma Sharp	200
Charlotte Crawford	201
Kelly Webster	202
Tyler Johnston	203
Nicole West	204
Ruth Prophet	206
Cameron Moore	208
Kasha Pow	209
Hannah Prophet	210
Laura Barry	212
Garry McInnes	213
Jennifer Graham	214
Gordon Campbell	216
Nicola Aitken	218
Sarah Trotter	220
Kirstie MacMorran	222
Louise Bell	223
Laura Stewart	224
Andrew Dixon	225
Rachel Kirk	226
Gavin Brown	228
Sarah Grant	229
Sara McConnell	230
Laura Johnston	232
Ross Kinnaird	234
Sean Rands	235
Shannon Hurst	236
Claire Mackie	237
Christopher Smith	238
Stacey Skelton	239

The Stories

A Day In The Life Of A Dog

Woke up, had the leftovers of what humans call breakfast. Then all the people went out to work or school. Then I just lay about the house and had a little doze off.

Then the big man came home for what he calls lunch. It's a pity I don't get any. The big man took me for a small walk around the corner and back.

Then the small man came home from school, he had a snack and watched TV which I don't really understand but I suppose I could watch a bit of cartoons.

Then after everyone was home, I have to sit in my basket while the people have dinner, yum, yum dinner, my favourite time of day, meat and flakes otherwise pedigree.

Soon after I had my dinner, I went outside to have a run about, I tried to chase the birds away and luckily I did.

When I went back inside, a while later, I went to the front room and lay about the place.

The big man took me out for a walk and I ran after three lady dogs. They were all much younger than me and I did not catch one! I went home with the big man and felt sad. To cheer myself up I spent the whole evening chewing the big man's slippers before I fell asleep and went into dreamland, ready to start a new day.

Michael Anderson (10)
Beaconhurst School

A Day In The Life Of An Ant

All day I've been work, work, working up and down the ant motorway as a punishment for not working hard enough. We have to have gathered one hundred and twenty leaves and if there is one short, we get executed.

At last it's the end of the day. I of course, got one hundred and twenty exact but Larry who's my best mate, got only one hundred and nineteen so he's getting executed.

The next day we got to work sharpish. We have to make the guillotine for the execution.

By the end of the day the guillotine is finished.

Flip who's very bloodthirsty, thinks this is a historic moment and will be remembered forever but as for Donny, he's been crying the whole morning and me, well I've just tried to keep my head on about it.

The day of the execution is going fine so far, the crowds are gathering and Donny's been sick seven times already.

The execution is starting and the crowds cheer.

'Are there any questions before I go ahead?' said the executioner.

'Can I keep the head?' asked Flip.

'What are you going to do with it, hang it on your bedroom wall?' said the executioner sarcastically.

'Yeah, great idea I hadn't thought of that' replied Flip.

The guillotine was about to go down and I jumped out of my seat and got my arm caught in the blades.

I went to bed that night. I woke up and I was a human.

Amy Rebecca Hilton (10)
Beaconhurst School

A Day In The Life Of Michael Owen

Michael Owen is one of the best footballers in Liverpool. First he gets up and has a wash. Then he then has his breakfast and watches television.

Next he goes to Anfield ground and has a talk with his manager and practices his football for tomorrow's big match against Barcelona. The team flies to Barcelona and plays them.

After the final whistle had gone, Liverpool cheered because they had won 3-2. They collected the cup and went to get changed, then they went to have a look around the shops. Michael Owen also likes girls. Michael Owen also goes to see children who are ill. He has six Liverpool strips

Two weeks after Liverpool played Everton and won 4-2. Heskey and Fowler were injured and they won't heal for two weeks.

Michael Owen likes CDs by Britney Spears and has posters on his bedroom walls.

He was charged for speeding.

He watches lots of television and listens to lots of music. He also likes shopping because there are cool bits and pieces and also likes writing letters to people and running his fan club.

Fraser Cormack (11)
Beaconhurst School

A Day In The Life Of Mary Thomson

It was a cold, wet morning at the stables and everyone was busy. Mary was sorting out all the clothes she would need while Annie, her groom, was sorting out the tack and everything else, plus the horse Mary would need for Badminton.

'Have we got everything Annie?' asked Mary, anxious to be off.
'Yes, I think so, who's driving?' said Annie.
'I will!' replied Mary.

At last, they were on the road and heading for Badminton. When they arrived, they made sure William was comfortable, they went to walk the cross country course.

Annie tacked William up and Mary warmed him up, ready to start.

Then she went into the arena for the first challenge - the dressage test!

'Good luck Mary!' shouted Annie.

Thankfully it was a good test.

The scoreboard had Mary at the top, but not for long. Next was the cross country!

She was halfway round the course, when William stumbled and fell. Mary shot out of the saddle and landed badly on her hand! Somehow, she got back on and finished the course.

Her hand was agony but she still had to do the show jumping. But could she?

The pain was awful but William took her round.

At the end everyone was cheering like mad. She didn't realise that she had gone clear in the fastest time!

She waited for the announcement wondering who had won . . . and it was her name called out, she couldn't believe it!

It was the best day in her life, her dream come true! That's my dream too!

Caitlin Stokes (10)
Beaconhurst School

A Day In The Life Of A Golfer

There was once a golfer who would get the ball onto the green but then disaster. He would putt the ball (not properly) so hard, it would break the flag. He would then get sent off the course for vandalising the property. So this meant that he had been to about ten million courses all over the country and got sent off every one. He then asked Wolf Woods (Tiger Woods' brother) what he was doing wrong. Wolf said you have to not hit it so hard. When Ted (The golfer) got back, he tried to not hit the ball so hard.

To everyone's amazement he got the ball in the hole the first time without breaking the flag. He then decided to do a tournament with the person who taught him, Wolf Woods. Ted thought he would lose. He won the whole competition and he nearly broke one flag but his caddie gave him the correct club just in time.

When he got the cup he said 'This is the first time I have won anything.'
Everyone laughed. From then on, he would always be asked 'How did you win it?'
After a long time he had realised what he had done wrong, he had forgotten to use his putter but that was his secret. The only person he's telling is you, but remember now it is your secret, so keep quiet about it!

Stuart Mackay (10)
Beaconhurst School

A Day In The Life Of Florence Nightingale

As the sun rises and breaks the darkness, the dew on the grass is sparkling like stars, a man in an army suit is walking along the field, picking up bits of dew on his boots and then kicking it into the air as he walks on the bloodstained grass and exploded mines around him. He kicks over bodies to find some life.

He climbs the fence to the next field in front of him and before he or I knew it, the man is dead, lying in front of me as I write this.

I go through this sort of thing every day, I wake up to the sounds of bombs in my ears, I enjoy this life though, looking after people, helping them if you like. Although my life is tough, I manage to like it.

'Miss this man's foot needs seeing to!'

Like I said, I do a lot of things, but it does good.

'There bandage that up and lay him over there!'

Then I went out to the deserted battlefield out the back, it was a fine day, unfortunately some planes were flying over, so I'll need to be careful, I checked everybody, but nothing.

Fact: If you didn't know, Florence Nightingale was a nurse during the Crimean War in 1853 - 1856. This war was against Russia and Turkey, France and Britain.

She was known as the Lady of The Lamp as she walked past the soldiers' beds checking them at night with a lamp.

Kirsten Lyall (11)
Beaconhurst School

A Day In The Life Of A Dolphin

'Hi! I'm Airlie and I'm a dolphin. I am here because I want you to learn more about dolphins!

First is breakfast, my mum Anna has got my breakfast. I have my mum's milk and I try a little bit of fish, then I go and try and find Kenny my cousin. He is only two weeks old and I need to be good to him.

Did you know?
Dolphins are just like people. They can be huffy like teenagers or as innocent as a three year old. They are also very intelligent.

Suddenly, a figure moves through the water. My mum makes sure that I am with her. Sharks! I can blend into my mum so that it looks as if we are one. Unfortunately my aunty Vera is too slow and the sharks ram into her.

Did you know?
A dolphin can kill a shark the same as a shark can kill a dolphin.

Next is my lunch. I eat fish and find it yummy. Kenny is still totally on milk. I start wishing I could walk on two legs because it must be cool.

Did you know?
Dolphins and whales used to have two legs and they walked on the earth, that was before they adapted to water.

In the afternoon I leap out of the water with my mum and play with my cousin Kenny until I am really, really tired.

I'm lucky I don't need to have a bath before I go to bed.

That's about all from me. So I hope you know more about dolphins.

Bye!

P.S. Dolphins are endangered and you can support us by sending money to WDCS.

Thanks and please help us.

Airlie the dolphin.'

Julia Summers (10)
Beaconhurst School

A Day In The Life Of A Bug

No there's nothing. I popped my head out the hole to see if there was anything there, I scuttled out a bit. I went down the hall into the next room and being a bug that takes you a while. Suddenly before I knew it, a giant vacuum cleaner came towards me. What was I to do? I mean I'm a bug.

So here I am inside a vacuum cleaner. How am I going to get out? I ask myself, because I am not going to survive in here. Oh no, I'm moving, I wonder where I'll end up?

The dustbin. I'm in a dustbin. Just great. Now I have to think of a plan to get out of here! Yes, I'm going to die. Ouch. That dog knocked me over. This isn't my lucky day but at least I can escape now, off I go down the corridor.

I have found a good spot, I think I'll sit down here, so I start to fall asleep. Bam! I work out I am sitting right in front of a speaker and I go flying in the other direction. So now I don't know where I am. I can't think of anything to do. I know, I'll explore.

After a little while I work out I had explored this room yesterday. I think I'll go back to my hole. Nearly there now. A shadow comes over me, then splat, welcome to my new life in Bug Heaven.

Aileen McDonald (10)
Beaconhurst School

A Day In The Life Of The Prime Minister

I got up very early because I had a busy schedule today. Following breakfast I had my first meeting with my cabinet ministers and advisors to confirm the plans for today and also the forthcoming election.

I flew to Cumbria to see the soldiers about the foot and mouth crisis, then it's on to Northern Ireland, to give a talk on the troubles there, in front of the Assembly.

After that on to America to see and speak to the Motorola chiefs about the job losses in Scotland and try to get their jobs back.

It's time to go back to London and have another meeting with the leaders of the foot and mouth crisis and then debate this and other matters before parliament closes for the day.

It's now time to go home briefly, have dinner and put baby Leo to bed.

Next I have to attend a press conference to update newspapers and television about the foot and mouth crisis with the latest figures and the new Government policy regarding slaughter because Phoenix the calf has survived for five days without its mother.

Home now to say goodnight to the older children.

I then went next door to meet Gordon Brown, to discuss plans about the new trust funds for babies, so that all the children in the future will be able to afford higher education or a starter home for themselves.

Finally it's time to return home, go to bed and prepare for tomorrow. Goodnight Britain.

Euan Lawrence (10)
Beaconhurst School

A Day As A Feral Cat

Opening one bleary eye, I find myself lying in a pile of dewy leaves. It's warm with a light breeze and my coat is muddy and wet. I start to groom it, but my kittens are crying for milk. They begin to suckle - their poor little bodies close to mine. Five tabby, four of them kittens. It is too risky. What if the humans come and take them away?

I must find food. As I pad down behind Pathfoot, two students walk towards me. They are giants, as all humans are, but they have food. They call it a burger and throw it down, wasteful, but generous. Snatching it up, I carry it into a shadowy corner and eat it. The burger is still hot, I tear it apart leaving the green vegetable, but I must find more food. Am I dreaming or can I heard a slight gnawing, nibbling then a squeaking? Yes! I'm getting ready to pounce.

I have the little mouse, it is dead. I have now bitten its head off, poor thing. Kittens, I need to move them, running back to my kittens I see them curled up sleeping, wait, there is a blanket under the leaves. I will drag them under the rhododendron bush by the lake, it is warm under there. Wow! My kittens are heavy!

I have finally got to the rhododendron bush and they are still asleep, but well hidden. I'll chase the ducks. There is a big fat one waddling by unaware of me because I am hiding so well. It is dusk now and the big fat one is drowsy. I pounce but it flaps onto the lake, curses! Ah, another mouse, I've got it. It's dead . . . yum! To the bush now, I am drowsy. That mouse tasted of burger. My eyelids are closing, lower and lower. What a day!

Charlotte Wylie (10)
Beaconhurst School

A Day In The Life Of Skye

Skye knows it's time to get up when the cockerels starting crowing but the problem is it is now 4.00am when she sneaks up to my room. 'Nice bed,' she says as she wiggles under the downy having given me a face wash. She knows that she has to hide because Mum says 'No dogs upstairs.'

When I get up, she goes outside and then she has breakfast. She loves food, and she spends most of the day on her back legs with her front up on the units, seeing if she can pinch any food.

After breakfast Skye likes a short game of football and a run round the fields. It's time to let the hens out. '*Great!*' says Skye 'Cockerel chasing is a great game.' After Mum comes out and puts a stop to this, the next challenge is to sneak out of the kitchen and find a comfy bed to lie on with something to chew.

After another row from Mum, she comes with us on a trip to the village. She likes the front seat and tries to make me move.

On the way home, we let Skye out at the bottom of the drive. A race with the car now takes place. When we get home, she has a quick hen chase, supper, another play and it's time for bed.

Max MacBeath (10)
Beaconhurst School

THE PERSON WHO INSPIRES ME

I have many inspirations but Fabien Barthez inspires me. The reason I like him is because he's a goalie and so am I. Fabien plays with Manchester United, they are one of my favourite European football teams. I think Fabien Barthez started his football career like me, playing with a boys' club. I play with Motherwell Colts.

Everyone in my family thinks Barthez is a good goalie, but I like him the most. I think Barthez is the best goalie in the world. I'm going to be the best goalie in the world as well, but I'll be better than him. I'm not saying that Barthez is a bad goalie, I'm just going to be the best.

I'm going to try harder in goal to get picked up by a youth team. I can't wait till I'm older to become a great goalie. My dad always tells me not to think too far into the future as I'm still only ten, but I like to think into the future.

It's amazing how time can fly but sometimes time doesn't fly and five minutes can seem like forever. I find it very hard when time takes forever. That's my inspiration.

Chris Tollan (10)
Calder Primary School

What Inspires Me

When I was about six years old, I started thinking about the Royal Navy. It was bought my attention when I saw an advert on the television. The advert was asking people to join the Royal Navy or the TA - Territorial Army. That's when it went through my mind that I wanted to join the Army. From that day on, I've watched many war films like The Great War, World War One and Two and lots more. I can't wait anymore, I wish that I was 18 so I could join.

3 years later I asked my dad about the Army, he said 'If you join the Army, it isn't as good, as you only get to go to one country in the world, if you stay for about 15 years,' at that moment my dad finished speaking. The Army went out of my head, and in went The Royal Navy, I had to be good at my maths and I must take orders. When I'm 12 I will try and join the cadets. When I'm 18 I will try to join The Royal Navy, it won't be easy as there will be lots of tests. I hope to be very famous and remembered in the Royal Navy.

That's what inspires me - The Royal Navy.

William Winnie (11)
Calder Primary School

SOMEONE WHO INSPIRES ME

Hi, my name is Thomas Grier. I have short orange hair, blue eyes and freckles and the person who inspires me is Barthez, the Man Utd goalkeeper. I think he is one of the best goalkeepers they have had in two years.

Barthez has blue eyes and he has got a 'baldie'. I think he is in his thirties. He absolutely loves playing with Man Utd, he wouldn't even leave for a million pounds in cash. Would you? Because I would!

Barthez has inspired me since I've known him. He inspires me because I am a goalkeeper and so is he. I like him because he is one of the best in the English Division and I know that for a fact. There is no doubt about it. I feel as if I am going to be better than him some day. Well, I hope I will be one of the best in Scottish League, if I have confidence in myself and most importantly, I have to stick to it.

If someone was in the twenty-five yarder, I would dive to their feet, then hit the ball as hard as I could. I have tried kicking the ball as high and as far as I could and I have accomplished my target of nothing scored past me.

If I join a team, I think I will be better than Barthez and that's who inspires me.

Thomas Grier (10)
Calder Primary School

The Person Who Inspires Me

I was five years old when I first heard of Stephan Klos. He is the best goalie ever I think. He's got skill, fast at running, good vision, saves goals and kicks the ball far. He's got blue eyes, brown hair, he plays with Rangers and he's quite tall.

When I'm older I want to be a goalie and I want to be like Stephan Klos. I like him because he is a goalie and plays with Rangers.

I am a goalie for a football team and if I want to improve my goalkeeping like Stephan Klos, I will just have to keep training to improve.

I've started two football teams and I am still training so that I can improve. I've been at one football team for four years and I've just started my school football team.

David Gray (10)
Calder Primary School

A Day In The Life Of Anyone Or Anything That Inspires Me

One month ago at Wrestle Mania X Seven, me and my dad were watching Chris Jericho crouch down and do a back flip to William Regal. Chris Jericho pinned William Regal and beat him. Chris Jericho had the title and Kurt Angle came to the ring. He hit Chris Jericho with the WWF Championship belt and did the ankle lock to Chris Jericho. William Regal got up and did the Regal Stretch. Chris Benoit came in and did the Crippler Crossface to Kurt Angle and Chris Jericho got up and did the Walls of Jericho to William Regal. All the referees were out trying to stop them from fighting. Vince McMahon came out and kicked Chris Jericho and Chris Benoit stood up straightaway and German Suplexed and then Chris Jericho did a move called the Lionsault. Chris Jericho did the Walls of Jericho to Kurt Angle and Chris Benoit did the Crippler Crossface to William Regal. Finally they let go and went backstage. I felt happy because I hate William Regal. I thought that he would get beaten up with weapons like steel chairs and chains, or get put through a table and he threw William Regal and Kurt Angle on to a truck.

Jamie Forrest (9)
Calder Primary School

She Inspires Me

I've always wanted to be a great singer and that's why I've chosen Ashley Dunne.

She's been on with Michael Barrymore and she sings on TV and in shows, all different kinds of stuff like that. She's quite small, but she has lovely blonde hair. She's in high school, I think it's the third or second year that she is in.

Ashley is the person I would like to be because since the day when she was singing Titanic in my school, I'd love to sing like her. Her voice is great.

I will have to stick with my choir practise every Wednesday and just try my very best. I have already been in a pantomime singing and I have entered for the choir in Cinders and also auditioned for the Music Academy and I've got in. Cool huh! There were only six of us who got in - Jennifer, David, Cheryl, Amiee, Jamie and I.

I absolutely love singing, I was bought a karaoke machine for Christmas and I sing with it nearly every day. So I want to be like Ashley Dunne because she's got a great voice and you should definitely try to catch her when she's on TV. There's nothing left to say except that she inspires me.

Nicola McAleenan (10)
Calder Primary School

They Inspire Me

They are one of the longest girl/boy bands in the world. There are three girls and two boys and their newest single is Here And Now. Lisa, Lee, 'H', Claire and Faye are *Steps!*

Lisa Scott - Lisa has medium length brown hair, blue eyes and light red lips. Her younger brothers are in a band called 3Scott-Lee's. Lisa is from Wales.

Lee Latchford Evans has short brown hair, brown eyes and light pink lips. He doesn't have any brothers or sisters. Lee is from south England, I don't know which city though.

Faye Tozer has short blonde hair, Mediterranean blue eyes and dark pink lips. She has a younger sister called Emily. Faye is from eastern England.

'H' has short blond hair, light blue eyes and light pink lips. He is very wacky. His real name is Ian Watkins. He is from Wales.

Claire Richards has blonde hair down to her shoulders, light green eyes and dark red lips. She comes from London.

They have been big pop stars for four years now and their first song was 5, 6, 7, 8. I think everyone's favourite was Tragedy, but my favourite would have to be the solo Faye sings on the album Steptacular which is called 'When You Took Your Love Away'. My favourite member of the band would have to be Lisa, because she inspired me to grow my hair and to sing a lot out loud. She has the sweetest voice I have ever heard.

Amanda Goldie (10)
Calder Primary School

WHO INSPIRES ME?

The person who inspires me is Kym Marsh from 'Hear'say'. She is twenty-four years old and has black hair. She was born and brought up in Wigan.

Myleene, Suzanne, Noel and Danny are the other people in the band.

Their very first single called 'Pure And Simple' was a hit record and they have sold the most singles of a first record.

When I am older I would like to be like Kym because she is great at singing and dancing and is in a very popular pop group. She also inspires me because she got a place in the band out of so many people and she kept on trying until she got a place. Kym had recorded a record when she was a teenager but wasn't successful.

I go to a lot of dancing, acting and singing clubs. I enjoy doing shows with my friends. I started dancing, acting and singing when I was about four and I've kept going ever since. When I am older I would like to go in for some auditions, like she did, and then I might get into a band and be famous.

When I am older I hope to be just as good, or even better, than Kym Marsh from Hear'say.

Francesca Flynn (10)
Calder Primary School

WHO INSPIRES ME?

Since I was five years old I have been inspired by art because I am great at drawing. I find art fun.

Art inspires me because it's fun drawing and I might become an artist. Maybe if you're an artist, it would be great and exciting.

I will get better at art if I keep practising, but I know I don't need to practise because I am already great at art. When I am older I might be an artist. Nearly all my family are great at drawing, when I was little I wanted to be an artist but now I don't know what I want to be. In my bedroom I have lots of pictures I have drawn. Nearly everyone in my street have asked me to draw Tigger for them.

I have so far drawn pictures and posters with lots of drawings on them in my class and I have art on Fridays. When I was in Primary 5, Miss McLuckie asked me what I was going to do with my drawing when I am older. But I said I didn't know, I always draw pictures in my homework and class jotters.

When I am older I am planning to have two jobs. Maybe like a vet and an artist. Soon I might change my mind and just be a vet because I am more interested in becoming a vet than an artist.

Alison McBride (10)
Calder Primary School

He Inspires Me

My name is Joshua Hill and I have blond hair and brown eyes. My dad's name is Andrew Hill and that is who inspires me. He has black hair, very short and he has blue or brown eyes, I can't tell which because I haven't focused on them yet. He inspires me because he plays football when he comes home from work and I like football, I am in a football team.

My dad's job is being a truck driver for Iceland, he has to get up at half-past two in the morning, and he drives long hours, and he comes in at half-past five. I would like to do that when I'm older, and I will try and achieve this level and try and get a better education. I will try to improve my development. When I do something wrong, he supports me.

My dad likes gardening and I like to help him when he is gardening. We sometimes go out and fish and talk. Sometimes my mum will pick my dad up in the car and I go with her to see my dad. Sometimes on Saturdays, he will go and watch football.

My dad likes to play on the computer with me, he likes to play football games on the PlayStation. At night he goes to his bed early because he gets up very early for work in the morning. There would be other jobs that I would like to do.

Joshua Hill (10)
Calder Primary School

INSPIRATION

Books like Harry Potter, Point Horror, Sweet Valley JR High, High and Twins all inspire me.

If I open a book and read a little I can imagine a picture in my head, but it's not just books that inspire me as you will find out if you read on.

Joanne Rowling's Harry Potter books inspire me so much! They are totally indescribable, I can't read a few chapters and then put it down, I have to read the whole book (they're that great!). I like them because of the words, the spells, poems, basically everything about them.

So far I'm at level C/D in writing and I've set a goal for myself, I'll keep writing stories, poems and songs.

I am also inspired by Kym from Hear'say. I mean, for her to have the guts to stick out through all those auditions and not give up. I have set a goal for myself there, I will stick at the theatre school I'm at, keep doing shows and then wait and see.

I'd like to be a singer, dancer, actor or author. I have set myself a goal for each of these, so now all I have to do is wait and see which suits me best.

Until then, I'll keep trying.

Danielle Hume (10)
Calder Primary School

A Day In The Life Of Anyone Or Anything That Inspires Me

The person I would like to be looks like this:

Long brown hair, a kilt, a sach, and a type of boot. His name is William Wallace. He lived in Scotland many centuries ago. His father and his brother went out to fight the English, but unfortunately his father and brother both died. So his Uncle Argyle came and took him away to his country. When he got older he went back to Scotland where he had lived when he was a wee boy. His father's friends came and asked him to go to a meeting about an attack on the English. So he went but on the way he saw a wedding celebration, his friend Hamish was there and he had a bit of a challenge. Hamish said that he wasn't William Wallace, and said that he could squash him like a worm. So William picked up a stone, walked forward and stood there, Hamish threw a rock and it went over William's shoulder and missed him, then William aimed his stone towards Hamish and threw it and hit him on the head and he fell. William helped him up and Hamish got up and said 'Welcome home!' Two days later his friends and army were fighting the English and they won.

But now I have to miss a part out and you're at the last battle.

So the first team of Scots, then the English, then William Wallace's team came and they met up and decided that some of the team should come in at the end. All William's team went to the front and they had made spears so that when the English horsemen came riding over very fast, William's team would stick out their spears; then they all started fighting with swords.

They fought and fought and just then the English were winning, but then the other team came and fought for William and won.

That night William got caught and the next day he was half-drawn and quartered, so he died.

William Boal (10)
Calder Primary School

A Day In The Life Of My Gran

My gran is 65 years old and lives with her husband, my grandpa in a small flat in Airdrie.

My gran would be quite fit if it wasn't for a tragedy of nature. In her early fifties, my gran was taken ill and had to go into hospital many times to get x-rays, blood tests and all sorts of things. The results did not turn out good and the tests showed that she had MS (Multiple Sclerosis). This disease makes it difficult for her to walk, so she has to use a walking stick just to get around her small flat and when she goes out, she has to be pushed in a wheelchair.

The thing that makes my gran inspire me is that every day since my gran found out she had MS, she sits in her small flat, either watching telly or reading magazines or newspapers, watching the days go by. She only gets out every so often every month and sometimes my gran's health goes down and she gets worse. But every Saturday when I go to see my gran and grandpa she is always happy to see us and smiles, even though she doesn't feel like smiling and tries to be as cool as any other gran!

My gran is the best gran, even though she can't do some things other grans can.

Victoria Swann (11)
Calder Primary School

A Day In The Life Of A Fire-Fighter

Personally I am awe-inspired by these extremely brave and selfless men and women who, on a daily basis, risk life and limb to save others from the raging and ruthless beast that is 'fire'.

Mark Eugene Quatrane woke up on the 2nd of May when his alarm clock rang at 8.00am (as usual). Mark was the Deputy Sergeant of the 54th Squad of the FDNY (Fire Department of New York) and he loved his job.

He swung himself out of bed lethargically, but when he thought of the huge fried greasy breakfast waiting for him at the Firehouse, adrenaline seemed to rush into his bloodstream. Mark was extremely fit, due to the physical exertion of his career, but if a man was going to toil all day, he needed a nutritious meal.

Mark's apartment was a large open-plan homely place, where he could relax after a hard day's work. After making coffee, he walked down the street to the Firehouse. It was pretty handy living so near his place of work.

When he walked in he was greeted by his friends Eddie and Mike. The high-pitched wail of the fire-alarm struck Mark's eardrums as he was only halfway to the breakfast table. 'Oh man!' thought Mark as he yanked on part of his fire-suit. He was first to dive down the pole.

All in a day's work for a fire-fighter.

Christopher Saunders (11)
Calder Primary School

A Day In The Life Of Anyone Or Anything That Inspires Me

The thing that inspired me the most was when I got a new pet guinea pig called Chocolate Chip (Chip for short). When I got Chip she was still very small, but also very lively.

When we got home I took Chip out of the box and put her in the hutch with Tufty, my other guinea pig, whilst I tidied up the hallway and then went to get Tufty and Chip.

When I tried to take Chip out, Tufty squealed and jumped in front of Chip.

'What on earth is Tufty doing?' I thought
'Hey, she's protecting her!' I said to myself.
'They are already firm friends' I exclaimed.
'Mum, come and help me take Tufty and Chip into the hall to watch them' I called.
'Alright!' she called back.

When we got Tufty and Chip into the hall, I watched for a very happy long time and then put them back. I felt especially pleased and now I don't just look at people and take them for granted, I try to find out about them, as much as possible.

Rebecca Sellar (9)
Calder Primary School

A Day In The Life Of Anyone Or Anything That Inspires Me

A day in the life of someone who inspires people, starts in my home.

Three days ago my mum and dad and my little sister and I were supposed to be watching our Saturday Night Special 'Who Wants To Be A Millionaire?' I was just coming out of my room when my little sister was calling me names. I ignored her and walked down the stairs. When I got down, my mum and dad told me to get straight back up the stairs to clean my room. My mum told me that my room was in a big mess. My dad told me if I didn't clean my room, I wasn't going to watch 'Who Wants To Be A Millionaire?'

So I ran back up the stairs and went into my room. My mum was telling the truth, it was a real mess. I had to get the vacuum cleaner and an air freshener out. I folded my clothes and put them away in drawers. I put my toys and my games in wardrobes and I told my mum and dad to come upstairs. They were amazed.

I was impressed myself, and my mum and dad were very pleased.

Gary McCombe (9)
Calder Primary School

A Day In The Life Of Anyone Who Inspires Me

The person who inspires me most is William Wallace.

William Wallace was a great hero in Scotland, his life was packed full of excitement, but I'm only going to write about one day.

It all began when the English wanted to fight the Scots, and there was only one man called William Wallace who wanted his freedom, so he decided today was the day. He got his friend who was called Hamish who also wanted his freedom, and the two of them were going to stick together. So they sat round the village until they heard the Englishmen coming into the village.

The Englishmen came raging into the village, all the children ran to their mums and the rest of the men decided they would fight, so they all got their swords and went into battle.

The battle was long but William Wallace knew he was not going to give up. All of the women and children watched, hoping this was the day when they all got their freedom for life.

William Wallace shouted 'Stop the battle, we the Scots only ask one thing, so please hear us out. Let us have our freedom, just one thing that's all we ask.'

But the English were determined to fight, so the Scots had no choice but to battle on. A lot of Englishmen were dying, so they decided to stop and that meant that the Scots had their freedom.

So now you see why he inspires me? Because he would never give up. Most people would, and when you read this story, hopefully you will remember how brave he was.

Lynsey Wilson (10)
Calder Primary School

A Day In The Lie Of Anyone Or Anything That Inspires Me

Last year I went to Spain for two weeks. I stayed in a hotel and I went to Barcelona Stadium to watch Barcelona versus Valencia.

Then it started - Rivaldo passed to Overmars, he passed to Lous Figo and was fouled but he got a free kick. Rivaldo took it, he tried a fancy shot and shoots. What a goal! The crowd roared with delight.

Barcelona 1 Valencia 0, the goalie kicks the ball out. Quadea shot at the goal, he scored. One each. Hesp passed to Figo, he hit it up to Overmars who crossed the ball to Rivaldo, he shoots and scores. The crowd shouted 'You're not singing anymore!' The goalie misses, kicks the ball and scores an own goal 3 - 1 and the half-time whistle blows.

Now they're back on again. Figo shoots crossbar and Rivaldo comes in for the header. Goal 4 - 1. I was very excited to see Barcelona win 4 - 1. Figo's shot hit the post and the man of the match was Rivaldo.
The final whistle blew

The person who I was talking about was Rivaldo, he inspires me to score goals and not to be greedy with the ball and play football. Now I am in a football club because of him.

Chris Grier (9)
Calder Primary School

A Day In The Life Of Anyone Or Anything That Inspires Me

At dawn, the Spanish sun came through the window of the cramped shed where Carmel slept.

Crack! Carmel woke up with a start, it was a sound that sends a chill down your spine. The camels were in the sun, they had already been hooked up to the machinery and the cruel man kept hitting every camel, but none of them cried out in pain because they were used to it. Time dragged on for these poor creatures who were being tortured by the sun. These camels were sore, angry and hungry. Many camels had given in to this torture and fell asleep. But Carmel knew if she stopped she would not get anything to eat.

I came at 1.30pm to see the Vineyard, but the camels were being tortured and I wanted to help them, I really did, but the guide said we couldn't go in. I was very upset so I jumped over the fence and went up to the man who was whipping them and said '*Stop it!*' The man replied by saying 'I won't!'

I went to Carmel, who was exhausted by the heat and very hungry. I gave her a stroke, she snickered a bit, so I stroked her some more as Carmel liked it. Suddenly Carmel kicked the cruel man and bit him. I untied the other camels who fell asleep after five minutes. This story says that you should treat animals like people, and they will love you in return.

Fiona Harrison (9)
Calder Primary School

A Day In The Life Of Anyone Or Anything That Inspires Me

Last year, in my house, my dad had to get up for another long hard day of work.

He has to get up at six o'clock every morning to get everything done. He has to get dressed and have his breakfast. Then at seven o'clock he gets me and my brother up. He makes our breakfast when all of us are up and helps us get dressed. Then it is time for work. He works in a window factory but my dad doesn't work with the windows, he works with computers. He works from eight o'clock to half-past four.

When he gets home at half-past four he has to go right back out again because he has two jobs. His first job is at the window factory and his second job is fixing computers.

When he gets home from his second job he is glad to be home but he is still exhausted. He always has time to help me with my computer. That is the story of why my dad inspires me.

Gemma Lees (9)
Calder Primary School

A Day In The Life Of Neil Armstrong

I woke up in the morning wondering why I felt so excited! Then I came to my senses, it was the day when we would land on the moon!

I floated out of my chair and went to the controls, I looked out of the window and saw Earth. Green and blue with white patches where the clouds were. I tore myself away from the view and looked straight ahead . . . I saw the moon, my tummy felt like snakes were trying to get out, I was going to land on the moon that very evening.

The speakers suddenly crackled and a voice said

'Apollo Eleven, are you receiving me? Over!'
I answered 'I can hear you, what is it?'
The voice replied 'You are going to land on the moon two hours before we thought. You must get ready. Over and Out!'

I jumped up so suddenly that I hit Buzz and woke him up.

'What is it?' he asked.
I didn't answer, then Buzz said it a little bit louder,
I answered 'We are g-going to land on the moon, t-two hours b-before we thought.'

Buzz looked amazed, then Michael woke up and he saw me and Buzz looking at each other and asked 'What's up?'

Buzz looked away and said 'We're going to land on the moon two hours before we thought!' He jumped to the controls and started to make a course to the moon.

Buzz and I went down to the landing craft with our suits on. Michael was left in the spacecraft to control it when we were on the moon.

Buzz detached us and took us closer and closer to the moon. We landed with a bump and a whine from the motor as the door went down and then we saw the landscape of the moon. Big craters and small ones. I walked down and waited for Buzz to wave me off . . . It was a wonderful feeling, it was a free feeling.

Then I said ‘This is one small step for man and one great leap for mankind.’

Stewart Ireland (10)
Carradale Primary School

A Day In The Life Of A Horse

I woke up this morning and I saw the light green grass. I saw my mate sleeping late. The light green grass was nice! I heard my owner coming to groom me, I like getting groomed because I like looking good in the summer.

'Hi mate, you're up?
I've just been groomed, do I look nice?'

Oh here come some people, I wonder if they have any food. Yes, I love food, I like it when they give us food, it's always nice.
Oh yes, it's the afternoon we're going for a ride.

'I like going for a ride do you?'

I love it when she takes us for a ride with the children, it's so nice.

It's teatime, I am going to eat some grass, then I'm going for a walk up the field. After that, I'm going to sleep.

'Are you coming for a walk up the field?
We might get nicer grass and see some rabbits.
I saw one yesterday, it was black and white,
It was running away into the woods. There was a deer too.'

Jaide McMillan (10)
Carradale Primary School

A Day In The Life Of A Dolphin

Hi, I'm Lolly, I'm a trained dolphin. My trainers are called Joanna and Emma, they're really friendly. They tickle my tummy and it feels great. I'd doing a great big show today with my friend Bubbles and loads of people are going to be there.

I have to do somersaults, which is really hard, but I can manage it.

'Lolly, Bubbles!' said Emma

Yessss! it's breakfast time. Come on Bubbles. Joanna has got a huge big fish, she's going to give it to me. Come on, come on. Arrgh Bubbles, you would have to stick your nose in. Get out of the way. Come on throw it. Yesss, I caught it.
Na Na Na Na Na Na That's me done. I'm off. Bubbles is still getting fed, greedy, hmmph!

'Five minutes to go guys,' said Joanna.

I'm really nervous, there are lots of people out there.
There's my cue, I have to swim about with Joanna on my back. Easy, peasy! Then I have to jump up and Joanna will go flying off my back into the water. Then Bubbles takes over. We have to go through hoops, do somersaults and loads of other things. Then finally, we go under the water with Emma on my back and Joanna on Bubbles' back and come flying out of the water with them standing on our noses. Great isn't it? I'd better go . . . bye, bye.

Kirsty Black (11)
Carradale Primary School

A Day In The Life Of A Shark

I was looking for some food. I found a small crab to eat.

Hi! I'm a tiger shark, I am one of the world's dangerous sharks. I live in the South Pacific with my brothers and my mum and dad.

I went out to hunt for fish, I saw other sharks chasing a shoal, they were my friends. I helped, we cornered them between a rock, we caught half a dozen and I brought them home for my dinner.

I went out again with my dad and brothers, we sneaked up on a giant shoal of fish, we caught loads of fish and my mum came along to help.

It was turning winter and the water was getting colder. We met some other sharks and we swam for miles to hotter water and we lived there until the summer came again.

John Willis (10)
Carradale Primary School

A Day In The Life Of David Coulthard

I woke up one morning but it was very dull. I get a little bit concerned in case it rains. I have been staying in a huge hotel in Brazil and I just remembered it was the day of *The Grand Prix!* I felt a bit giddy. I ran downstairs and jumped into my blue McLaren.

I raced over to the three mile long track with the fast left and right corners. I was feeling quite lucky today and still a bit nervous. I had to park a long way away from the F1 garages. I ran up, out of breath and saw Mika was already there, talking to our Manager Ron Dennis. We went over some safety issues. Then we were on the grid. I was starting in pole position. The red were on and then off. I was off, as fast as I could because I knew Michael Schumacher was behind me. Michael went shooting past me. Nothing much happened until I started catching Michael and he went into the pits. I was very surprised but kept going faster and faster.

He came back out but I was long gone. I stayed at a steady pace until the finishing line in case I went too fast and went flying off the track. I was very happy but completely focused. I was on my last lap and Ron told me to take it easy. Just then my back-end stepped out and the crowd all gasped but I flicked it back on and kept going faster than ever. I passed the chequered flag.

We were up on the podium with Michael to my right and Pablo Montoya was to my left. I got the plaque and then the champagne came. I was on cloud nine. I went back to the hotel at 3 o'clock in the morning. I went to sleep.

Robert Mackinnon (11)
Carradale Primary School

A Day In The Life Of Danny Foster

I woke up this morning, feeling terrible, I could hear Noel sleep talking. I looked into the mirror and from behind I heard Noel saying 'Oh Danny, don't we look a right state in the morning.'

I thought he was still sleep talking but then I saw him in the mirror!

I went downstairs to see what the papers had come up with today! You'll never guess what they said, apparently this house we're in is a popstars prison but I quite like it. Oh no here comes the girls (Suzanne, Kym and Myleene) they are always moaning and look a right state in the morning. I told them about what the Sunday papers had brought today, they were in stitches laughing.

We're getting a visit from Nigel, Nicky and Paul today (oh in case you didn't know, they're the three judges who picked us!)

Oh they're here, I better go act the host! Nigel just told us about our first two gigs, the first is in Cardiff and the second is at the SECC in Glasgow. We're all so excited, it will be excellent, all our fans screaming for us, I can picture it now.

Noel's cooking dinner just now, it smells absolutely great. It's chicken curry and rice - beautiffffuuuuulllll! I love the way Noel cooks. He made lovely soups for lunch, we managed to scoff it before the judges arrived.

I'm eating my dinner at the moment, oopsie! Does it taste nice to you? I love it.

We're about to watch a video, it looks excellent, I must say this is one of my favourite days, ever!

Emma Dudley (11)
Carradale Primary School

A Day In The Life Of Robbie Williams

I woke up this morning to go and record another new single. I walked down to the recording studio and on my way there, I went into a cafe and got a cup of tea and a bun.

When I came out there was a crowd of fans but luckily the recording studio was just next door so I went in.

'Hi Robbie, it's 11.30 so we better get to work.'

It's now 1.30, I am done. We recorded one single but we had to do it four times so it was just right. I am now going to get my lunch. I will have a plate of chips and a coke. I am going down the gym after I've finished.

It is now 4.30 and I am going home to have my tea, I wonder what the cook has made.

'Robbie, is that you there?'
'Yes, what's for dinner?'
'Roast, veg and chips.'

It was lovely.

I am going to a party now, better bring some cans or we'll probably run out.

I have to pick up a few mates because they don't have cars.

Just back from the party, it was great, going to bed now, night, night.

Bryony Galbraith (11)
Carradale Primary School

A Day In The Life Of A Hunter

The alarm clock beeped and I got up like a shot and put on my clothes. I had a quick slice of toast and then I checked the loading bolt on my rifle because it was a bit faulty. Today I was going up to Crossaig to shoot deer.

I filled the magazine with cold, shiny bullets. I checked the sights and had to alter the crosshair slightly. I cleaned out the barrel with my pipe cleaning brush and then put it in the bag. I went out to my jeep and put it in the back. I took the four wheeler out of the shed and put it on the trailer.

I put the trailer onto the jeep and made sure it was safe. I returned to the kitchen and filled up the flask with hot, black coffee. I heard my wife shout goodbye and I shouted goodbye back to her. I grabbed my hat and shouted to my dog Butch and then headed out to Crossaig.

I passed the power station and then Grogport. When I got to Crossaig, I unlocked the gate and drove through, I jumped out and locked the gate. I dipped my feet in the foot and mouth disinfectant. I carried on till I got to the top of the hill. I lifted my rifle from the back seat, clipped the magazine in and jumped out of my bullet belt and then set off through the thick bushes. I came to the heathery plain beside the loch.

There were two baby roe dear but they were too small to shoot. Two mature sika stood at the top of a hill, I lifted my rifle to shoulder height and then put my eye to the sights. I got the crosshairs on the large chest of the bigger of the two, flicked the safety catch off and pulled the loading bolt back and then pulled the trigger slowly. The large sika fell to the ground.

Once I had got it home, I gutted it and skinned it.

Andrew Ramsay (12)
Carradale Primary School

A Day In The Life Of Michael Mols

I woke up one nice, sunny morning in my house in Glasgow and I remembered it was Sunday, the day for the big match Rangers vs Celtic.

I rushed out of bed and looked at my clock, it was 11.00am. I would have to be at Ibrox in one hour. I quickly ran to the cupboard and took out my Rangers top with Michael Mols printed on the back, then I took my shorts and socks and shoved them all into my bag. I ran to the kitchen and made myself some breakfast.

After my breakfast, I got my football boots and put them in my bag, then I ran outside and got into my Ferrari. I started the engine, then started to drive to Ibrox. After a ten minute drive, I got out of my car and looked at the giant stadium. Then I opened the door and I heard a loud cheer. Jorg Albertz, Kenny Miller, Steffan Klos and Fernando Ricksen were standing there looking at me and someone was behind me, it was Rangers' new player Tore Andrew Flo.

I shook his hand and said how happy I was to have met him, then Albertz said to me that he was happy to see me back from my injury.

Then we all walked to the changing rooms and I got into my football kit and walked to the dugout. We heard the cheering of the fans, then we started to jog to the centre spot and the referee blew the whistle.

We managed to keep possession but not enough to score but after 15 minutes, Albertz scored a free kick, then another goal came by me, thanks to Barry Ferguson. Then the ref blew the whistle for half-time.

After half-time, Celtic took centre, then after ten minutes, I scored a volley, then before I knew it, the whistle went. When I got in Dick Advocaat said how good I did, I then left and went home.

Michael Fee (11)
Carradale Primary School

A Day In The Life Of Anne Robinson

'Start the clock!'
'Mary, what currency does Denmark use?'
'Krones,' answered Mary.
'The correct answer was Danish Krones, but I'll accept Krones,' I said briskly.

The whole round went on like that. The team was good, I admit it but someone lost the team £250 making them just short of £1000.

Finally, everybody had finished scribbling.

'It's time to vote off the *weakest link*!' I cried.
Rufus was voted off, but he wasn't the weakest link.

It was now time for competition between the two survivors of the game. They had £7120 to fight for. They glanced fiercely at each other, daring each other to fight for the money. Audrey and Jody took a deep breath and looked at me. They were ready.

'Audrey was the strongest link in the last round, so she has the choice of who goes first,' I declared.
'I'll go first,' she answered.
'Let's play the *weakest link!'* I exclaimed.
'Jody, in science, what does DNA stand for?'
'Pass,' she shook her head sadly.
'The correct answer was deoxyribonucleic acid,' I said.
'Audrey, in geography, where is Newburgh?'
'Scotland,' she said.
'Correct,'

Next, I asked Jody:
'What currency does Poland use?'
She raised her eyes to the ceiling. She looked very hopeful.
'It's Zloty,' she said breathlessly.
'Correct,' I said. I felt confident for Jody, although Audrey was a big match for her.

In the end Audrey won, and that was the end of the day in the life of Anne Robinson.

Cait Kearney (11)
Elmvale Primary School

A Day In The Life Of Captain Kirk

The oxygen supply and the engine were operating accurately. The countdown started and then finished with an almighty crash and with it, I got tossed into a nearby computer. Several crew members helped me up. I said I was fine but Spock, my loyal friend and companion from my last expedition, said I must go and rest at sickbay.

When I got out of the claustrophobic sickbay, I decided to take a walk around my ship and I then heard a scream and I knew at once it was the . . . Klingons.

As I ran through the corridor, I noticed a map of the starship; several red lights flashed representing Klingons at the brain bay area where I know Scottie, also a loyal friend, was working. So I ran on, worried about my friend. I went into the weapon room and got a powerful weapon which could blow anyone's head off with one careless shot, then I ran to the nearest corner of the brain bay. I stayed there until help arrived.

Soon help did arrive. We could now attack. I had a strange feeling, we were too late. We pushed right through the closed door. We fought the battle and won it, although the Klingons did fight a good battle.

My feeling, as before, was correct. We were too late; our loyal and trusty friend Scottie was dead. Our expedition had only just begun and we had already experienced death on our ship, but we knew we had to let that pass and carry on bravely.

Rebecca Woodhouse (12)
Elmvale Primary School

A Day In The Life Of Tim Duncan

'I'm Tim Duncan and I'm about to go to the NBA2003 finals between us, the San Antonio Spurs and the Lost Angeles Lakers. We have only won once against the Lakers in 1999. I'd better go, it's 4 hours till the game.

I'm here at last in our home court in Texas with just 2 hours to go until the game. Here comes the coach.'

'Listen up team, here's how it's going to go. Tim you're going in for the first 2 quarters, David, you're going in for the whole game. As for the rest you'll be switched in and out the game. OK right, go and get ready!'

'It's time for the game.

Oh no we're losing. Wait, coach is signalling me on, I better go.

Yes, I've got the ball, we're only down 70-72. I could shoot a 3 point field goal and win the game. Here I go, I'm going to shoot. Yes! We win the game 73-72.'

Colin McCormick (12)
Glenburn Primary School

A DAY IN THE LIFE OF HARRY POTTER

Hi, I'm Harry Potter and today is the day I and the whole school have been waiting for, for months. It is the Quidditch Final between Gryffindor (the team I play for) and Slytherin (the team my arch enemy Draco Malfoy plays for).

In my opinion Quidditch is the best sport ever invented but others may disagree. It is played on broomsticks high in the air with four balls, but the rules are too complicated to explain so I won't, I'll just say that it is brilliant. Anyway, today Gryffindor will face Slytherin in the Quidditch Final. This is the first time in seven years that Gryffindor have reached the final.

I was the youngest player in a century (when I was in first year) to play for their house team and now I am in third year and I have the fastest racing broom in the world. My broom is a firebolt and I got it for Christmas from an anonymous stranger. It had to be checked for jinxes because everyone thought it was from Sirius Black who's A - supposed to be after me and B - my godfather, only I'm not supposed to know that he's my godfather. Oh, well I've got to go out onto the Quidditch pitch. I am sooooo nervous, but still excited about it.

I really need to win this because if I don't Malfoy will be too happy and I couldn't stand it if he was.

Hi, I'm back from the Quidditch pitch and guess what - we won! I can't believe it! I held the Quidditch Cup up for everyone to see and now we are going to party all night.

Laura Burns (11)
Glenburn Primary School

A Day In The Life Of Tweety Pie

On the 25th of May, at my house, I was sitting in my cage and Sylvester was lying, sleeping under me. Oh, by the way I'm Tweety Pie. I'm a little yellow bird with big blue eyes. Granny says I look cute.

Sylvester is a big black and white cat. Granny says he is a fat, lazy cat.

Anyway I was just sitting whistling a happy tune when suddenly my cage started rattling, I didn't realise that it was Sylvester until I saw his face staring up at me. I was holding onto my swing as tight as I could.

He started to clamber up the side of the cage, he opened the little door and reached in. A big, hairy paw grabbed me but I bit him and he let go in pain. He fell to the floor in agony. I shut my door and made a lock for it. I locked the door and lay in my bed. I was very cold and shocked. Granny came in and smacked Sylvester, but she gave me an extra blanket and some hot chocolate and put me to bed.

Leigh Nimmo (11)
Glenburn Primary School

A Day In The Life Of Bugs Bunny

I am Bugs Bunny, the TV character who is out of the programme Looney Tunes. I have friends called Daffy Duck, Tazmanian Devil and Sylvester. Sylvester is a cat and he chases Tweety Pie, Sylvester's owner is Granny.

Bugs Bunny went to a very creepy, scary castle. He was . . . scared out of his wits, it was at night and it was dark. Bugs Bunny had an idea to go and get the torch.

In the big grey castle, at the top of a big hill, it was the day time. The hill was covered with children playing football. Some of the children were playing tennis and some of the children were playing badminton.

Bugs Bunny got a big surprise when he got to the big castle because the big table was set for Bugs Bunny to have something to eat and something to drink like a glass of wine.

Kym Gilmour (11)
Glenburn Primary School

A Day In The Life Of Bugs Bunny

One day it was very sunny and the farmers were out doing their job. Bugs Bunny was still sleeping in his burrow and it was about 10.00 in the morning and all the people said: 'Wake up, come on it is morning time.'
So Bugs Bunny got up and he didn't know what to have for breakfast. He was thinking to get some carrots but he didn't have any left. He had to go down to the supermarket. So off he went to the supermarket and got about twenty odd carrots. Then he went to the checkout to pay for them and it was about £13.00 for all those carrots so he paid the money. Then he went back to his place for a carrot for breakfast and that was that.

Bugs Bunny felt like chasing all of the chickens and the farmer heard all of the noise and said, 'What is going on round there?'
Bugs Bunny always gets chased every time and he doesn't like it at all, so I suppose he'd better stop chasing everyone in the whole street. He went to complain to the council and they said 'I can't help you at all - but, but, but nothing thank you very much.'

Bugs Bunny had a terrible day.

Eilidh Cameron (11)
Glenburn Primary School

A Day In The Life Of Dick Advocaat

Wakes up, makes two phone calls, first to Bert Konterman to take me to training and second to see if Rivaldo will sign for 45 million and to see if Sunderland will swap Tony Vidmar for Don Hutchinson. The door rang, it's Bert Konterman. I quickly ate my breakfast and went into Bert's Ferrari. They were headed for training when Dick's mobile rang, it was Rivaldo's agent and said he would sign and will fly to Glasgow tomorrow. It was a massive boost, ahead of today's game with Celtic.

The training began, Bert Van Lingen was doing the training, I had a press conference about Rivaldo and if Hutchinson would sign. The press conference was very short, so he went back to training. The strikers were practising shooting. The mid fielders were passing and shooting and the defenders were winning corners, I was very confident about winning the game with Celtic, the game was at Ibrox.

Dick told the players the starting eleven, it was a 4-4-2, Klos was keeper. The four defenders were Ricksen, Moore, Konterman and Numan. The four mid fielders were De Boer, Ferguson, Van Bronckhorst and Albertz. Up front were Flo and Mols. I couldn't play Rivaldo because he hadn't arrived.

The game kicked off at a fast pace, Flo hit a shot which was brilliantly saved from Robert Douglas, then Celtic broke up the pitch and Klos made a great save from Larsson. Rangers won the game and Hutchinson signed, so did Gabriel Batistuta.

Chris Jardine (12)
Glenburn Primary School

A Day In The Life Of Britney Spears

Hi, I'm Britney Spears, I am a singer and I have brought out two albums. Each day is different for me. Today is a big day as I'm off to do a concert in Miami.

The time is five thirty in the morning and I'm going for breakfast, then for a dress rehearsal with the camera crew.

OK, I've earned a lunch break now. I'm beginning to get a little nervous, the crowd is beginning to file in now, there is supposed to be about ten thousand people here tonight and the front row seats are just about full.

The nerves are slowly but surely taking over me, I'm in the dressing room right now. My make-up is done and I'm nearly changed. It is six o'clock now and my concert starts at six thirty!

The time has come, I step out onto the huge stage and a roar sweeps over the audience. Then everything goes silent. The music has started now and I begin to dance and sing.

I have now finished my first song. My nerves die down but the enthusiasm of the crowd builds up.

Guess where I am now? Backstage! I'm finally finished, I think this has been one of my very best ever concerts.

Fiona Edmond (11)
Glenburn Primary School

A Day In The Life Of The Undertaker

I am a wrestler called The Undertaker. My brother Kane and I are the tag team champions. We beat Edge and Christian for the title at 'Raw is War'.

I was outside of the ring with Edge when Triple H and Stone Cold came out with steel chairs and laid into Kane's arm with them. Christian and I were in the ring, then I did my finisher called 'The Last Ride' to him, the pinned him 1, 2, 3 and we won the title.

We will play Triple H and Stone Cold tomorrow night for the tag team titles and it is a no disqualification match, so anyone can enter and start fighting, but nobody will come in. Kane and I were on the top ropes across from each other when Triple H and Stone Cold stood up and turned round. We did a flying clothes line and knocked them down again and pinned them 1, 2, 3.

We retained the title when Chris Jericho and Chris Benoit came and put the walls of Jericho and Crippler Crossface on Kane and I.

We didn't tap out because we got out of it and we did a double chokeslam, then a last tide to them when Regal and Angle came out and put the ankle lock on and the Regal Stretch on Bonoit and Jericho, then on Kane and I. We got taken to hospital and Angle and Regal got suspended for 2 months.

Kyle Thomson (11)
Glenburn Primary School

A Day In The Life Of A Vet

It was a normal day for me, waking up at half past seven to get ready for work. I got in my car at about quarter to eight to drive to the practice. It is only fifteen minutes away so I get there at about eight.

When I get there, I put on the white jacket and wash my hands, I called in the first patient, a rabbit called Dennis. His owner was worried about the length of his teeth and nails. They were quite long so I got out my clippers and cut his nails and teeth. I went to wash my hands again, but as I was doing that, an emergency came in.

I quickly wiped the table and looked at the St Bernard puppy called Benji. He wasn't breathing. His owner said he had something stuck in his throat. I called in my practise nurse, Fiona to put him on anaesthetic so I could get it out. I put Benji on the operating table.

I opened his mouth and slowly put a tube down his throat, that had a small camera on the end, so I could see what was stuck and then I saw it, it was a chicken bone.

I reached in and pulled it out, I put Benji in the recovery ward to recover. After that I washed my hands and the table, it was now about 12 o'clock. After lunch I had an injured squirrel and a hamster. I then went home to relax.

Gillian Sherry (11)
Glenburn Primary School

A Day In The Life Of S Club 7

One Friday night, us in S Club 7 were on our way down to Los Angeles to perform two hit singles. We were singing, Friday Night and Viva La Viesta. We were very excited.

But bad news was waiting for us, the concert had been cancelled because the concert didn't raise any money to pay the groups. When we got told this, we were very depressed. We were hoping to get back to England the next day. The night was very dark, very silent. Sirens went off in the background.

As every other famous star left in their cars and Mr Music left in his limo, we just stood there waving goodbye to everyone that passed us.

A while later, the only car that was left was the S Club car, as our 7 sad faces got in our red and white open top car, we went to our hotel and slept all night.

When we were ready in the morning and sitting in the sitting room, all with gloomy faces, I shouted out, 'What are we going to do? My mum, dad and family think I'm coming back today.'
'So does all of ours' answered Paul.
'You got that one right,' said Rachel.

Soon we got called in to say we were invited to a competition to sing our two songs.

The competition went well, in fact, very well. We got first place and we went back to England proudly because we won the World Champion Singing Group.

Laura Hepburn (7)
Glenburn Primary School

A Day In The Life Of Stefan Klos

I woke up at 9am and I had to rush to make it to training although I was already late, but as I had to go for a run around the block I was already warmed up. Then I set off for my football training. When I arrived I had to listen to Dick Advocaat, my manager, yap on saying that I should always be here in time. Today we were in the Scottish Cup final against Celtic, who have already won the league.

We were all in the dressing room listening to the formation we were to play. Barry Ferguson as usual never listened to what the manager had to say. Then the game started and the fans went wild.

Barry Ferguson hit the crossbar with a header but then managed to mess up smart in defence when Henrik Larsson took the ball off him and scored past me. But he managed to come good again when he scored past the Celtic keeper and made it 1-1. It stayed like that until the final whistle went, so it had to go to extra time, then penalties. In penalties, Barry Ferguson scored the 5th penalty and I saved the last penalty and got the cup. We all took turns at lifting the cup but when I lifted it, I got the biggest cheer.

When I went back to get changed, in the dressing room, my mobile went off, it was Barcelona wanting to know if I wanted to join them. I said, 'I could never leave this team.'

Dick Advocaat was proud of me.

Stuart Barr (11)
Glenburn Primary School

A Day In The Life Of A Wrestler

Hi I'm WWF wrestler Chris Jericho and I have to get up at 7.00am and go to the Texas Astrodome for my wrestling show to perform.

When I get there, I warm up and stretch, then I head for the gym where I meet the other wrestlers.

The show starts and our boss Vince McMahon makes the matches, I had to take on William Regal in a Tables, Ladders and Chairs match for the IC belt, it is where I have to climb the ladder and take the belt.

Then the match started and I had the IC belt to start with, I picked up a chair and hit William Regal with it seven times. I then set up a table and sat William Regal on it. I ran to do a moonsault but I missed and I went through it. The table was thrown out of the ring and I went to the top rope and spinning heel kicked the chair in William Regal's face.

My special move is the Walls of Jericho and I put it on him.

I set up the ladder and climbed it and I then got the belt and won the match, my job was done. I went backstage and got changed and set off home.

Mark Porter (12)
Glenburn Primary School

A Day In The Life Of Barry Ferguson

I woke up at 8.30am. I got up and went for a shower, then I got changed. At 9.00am my agent phoned me and told me I had a press conference at 10.30am at Ibrox. I had to hurry because at 2.00pm I had to fly out to the San Siro for the UEFA Champion's League Cup Final.

My agent told me he would come and pick me up for the conference. At 9.30am my agent came and picked me up, I was living in Glasgow so it was not far to Ibrox. When I got there, the press were already there. The conference went fine, then I went back to my house and got packed. We all met up at the airport.

There was not a lot of press there, we all got checked in and we had to wait for twenty minutes. Dick Advocaat the manager of Rangers was very confident.

Then we got on the plane, we were not on it for long, when we got to Italy, we got through the airport quickly. We went to our hotel. Then we went for a small training session at 4.00pm. The game was at 8.00pm.

We went for dinner. We had pasta because that gives us a lot of carbohydrates. Then it was time for the game Dick told us the team. When the final whistle blew it was one each. It went into penalties. We won the game. We were the Champions.

Alan Stevens (11)
Glenburn Primary School

A Day In The Life Of My Mum

What a nice morning. I'll just go and wake up Toni and her sister Bryony, it's time to get up now. Bryony's the youngest, she's only two. Charli, make your bed. Charli's nine. Toni go and make your breakfast. Do you want toast or cereal?

'I'll have toast please mum,' said Toni,
'Alright, but can you please make Bryony some cereal?'
'OK.'

My daughters are no angels but they can be a great help (sometimes). Charli has a scar on her face, (and a rather big one too) because when she was three, she was attacked by a dog. She had to have over fifty stitches. Bryony's always got a cold and Toni is just always complaining. Anyway I'll be back once I have a shower.

OK I'm back, I've washed my hair, dried my hair, brushed my teeth and got changed. Now I'll have to change Bryony and do the housework.

I have to go to work now. It's quarter to nine, so I'll drop Toni and Charli off at school and I'll be back at ten thirty. See you then.

I have to go to Mothers and Toddlers now. It's at the South Church.

'Hi Angela. Where's Emma?'
'Oh she's at home, sick. She's got the cold,' said Angie.
'Oh is she alright?'
'Yeah she just keeps sneezing,'
'On you go and play Bryony,'
'No!'
'Bryony always argues and if she doesn't get what she wants, she goes off in a huff.'

Time for tea and biscuits. Bryony will run one hundred miles an hour once she sees the biscuits. We go home in half an hour to watch Teletubbies and Tweenies. The rest of the day will be boring, I'll just stay in and watch some films.

Toni Currie (11)
Glenburn Primary School

NEIL ARMSTRONG

Hi, I'm Neil Armstrong. It was the day of the launch of Apollo 11, 20th July 1967. It was very early in the morning so we had a few hours to get ready for the mission.

First the suits had to be checked over for oxygen faults or anything else. It was about an hour to take-off to space. There were some more checks to happen on the actual spacecraft, and they took half an hour.

Right then the audience were filling to over 1000 people and it was time to enter the spacecraft. We were now on the craft and buckled ready to go. The countdown had started - 10, 9, 8, 7, 6, 5, 4, 3, 2, 1 - blast off!

We were now on our way to outer space. We had made it up to space. The moon was in our sights and we were really excited. We had now transported into the moon module in which we would touch down on the moon.

Now we were on the moon. I went out and picked up a sample of moonrock for the viewers down on Earth. After that we made our journey back down and the heat was very intense. We landed in the Pacific and everybody was waiting. We were heroes.

Kris Baillie (12)
Glenburn Primary School

A Day In The Life Of . . . A Catwalk Queen

4.00am my alarm clock bleeped,
'Up, up, up!'
7.00am. Stomach crunches, 600 sit-ups and 100 weight lifts, I mumble my daily routine.
'Then wax legs, pluck eyebrows and apply face mask and cucumbers to my eyes and face - then breakfast.'
Just then Mo walked in - he's my personal assistant. He's alright but he talks in a high voice and wears weird suits.

'Darling! What are you doing? You should at least be on your 400th stomach crunch! Chop! Chop!' he yelled.

'Breakfast! Yum, yum!' I say then I look at my plate, 'Muesli. Yuck!' I say to myself. I look at what Mo's eating. A huge, big, greasy fry-up! What I wouldn't give to have a bite of that crispy, meaty piece of bacon, I counted up the calories in my head. I couldn't, my whole career would be in jeopardy. I wolf down a few spoonfuls of muesli but I am too depressed to eat.

Later that day Mo and I took a taxi to the Vogue Magazine office for an interview with Sarah Celshaw. I'm starving. Mo had made me watercress, green bean and chestnut salad for lunch. I couldn't bring myself to eat it, for it tasted like feet!

We finally arrived at the Vogue office, Sarah greeted me and invited me up to a cosy looking room. 'Marge,' she said into a telephone at her desk, 'I'll have a cuppa and my guest' she said turning to me, 'Coffee, tea, cheesecake?'
I hesitated - I love cheesecake. Mo glared at me. I sighed. 'Mineral water will be fine thanks!'
'Marge, a mineral water and a tea for Mo and I.'

Marge arrived with my water, 2 teas and a huge slice of cheesecake for Mo. I nearly passed out. I haven't eaten more than 4 bowls of muesli in over a week. I wanted to eat Mo's cheesecake right there but I couldn't!

My dinner was watercress and celery soup. I force down a few spoonfuls. I do my nightly exercises, I phone my mum but I am still depressed. I sink into bed. Cakes and chips take over my brain. 'Get a grip!' I say drifting into a deep sleep.

Emma Durkin (11)
Glenburn Primary School

A Day In The Life Of Suzanne From Hear'say

On Thursday the 26th of April I was walking down the street with the rest of Hear'say. The band Hear'say has Danny, he has a great smile and has no hair. He usually wears jeans or cords and a T-shirt. Kym, she has two children, usually wears a fancy black top and black three-quarter length trousers and normal flat shoes. Noel has a good sense of humour. He usually wears soft trousers and a T-shirt. Myleene has brown fine hair and likes playing the piano. Finally me (Suzanne) - I have short, blonde hair that tucks into my face. I wear a little blue T-shirt, black trousers and black sandals. Anyway, back to Hear'say.

I was walking down the street with the rest of Hear'say and there was people shouting at us wanting autographs. We started running (we were already late) because we were on our way to a Top Of The Pops performance.

When we got there I started to get my make-up on. I had blusher, lipstick and eye shadow. I got my costume out, it was a really fancy top which was beige with a silver Chinese dragon on and blue trousers (leather). We were all dressed and set. We went out onto the stage and started singing. Everyone was singing perfectly but I realised it was a bit quieter than usual, then Noel nudged me and said 'Why aren't you singing Suzanne?'

Abbey Abrahart (11)
Glenburn Primary School

A DAY IN THE LIFE OF BONNIE PRINCE CHARLIE

'Hi and welcome to the Battle of Culloden. Today we are going to talk to Bonnie Prince Charlie. Oh, here he is now. Prince Charles! Prince Charles!'
'What? You know I'm a very busy man.'
'I know but . . .'
'But nothing, go away!'
'All right!'

We will talk to him later. Anyway for those who know about Bonnie Prince Charlie, he is a mad man who led or is leading the Jacobites. This is what he looks like. He has short, curly white hair, he has a green hat, a tartan cardigan and a white shirt. He is nice, although he can be grumpy.

Now might be a good time to talk to him. Let's go and see.

'Prince Charles can I . . .'
'Alert men! Retreat! *Retreat!* Sorry no time to talk!'

Bang! Bang! Bang! Bang! All the Jacobites were dead. Then Bonnie Prince Charlie ran away dressed up as a woman.

Natalie Pettigrew (11)
Glenburn Primary School

A Day In The Life Of A Giraffe

Faraway in the South of Africa there lives a seven-year-old giraffe called Coco. She has big eyelashes, browny-orange skin with dark brown spots on her. She lives with her owners Ern and Jake. She has lived with them for seven years now. They live way out in the wilderness where there is hardly any breeze and the sun beats down real hard, in South Africa.

Coco wakes up with the sun beating down on her long, slim neck and the air smelling fresh as ever.

'Coco, it's time for breakfast,' Ern says, coming out of the house to Coco's stable.

Coco rises from the stack of hay (her bed) walks over to Ern, and they walk over to the trees together. Coco stretches her long neck skywards and crunches into the crisp, green leaves.

'Crush, crush,' Coco munches. After Coco has had her breakfast, she and Jake head down to the lake for her to get some water and to get washed. When they get back, Coco, Jake and Ern go off into an open field of pure green grass with some corn here and there.

They play a game of football and head back home for lunch. Coco gallops against the wind and stops outside their field gate. She goes straight over to the trees and munches away quite happily. Ern and Jake go inside to watch television, while Coco runs around outside.

'Coco dinner is served,' Jake tells Coco.
Coco goes into her stable and on a high shelf is her favourite meal of carrots and cucumber. Coco is delighted.

After that Coco goes for a run round and to the lake for some water, then goes home to bed and has a wonderful dream.

Ainsley Fyfe (11)
Glenburn Primary School

A Day In The Life Of Solid Snake

In the cold, harsh climate of Alaska lives 'Solid Snake', formerly a member of Special Operations Foxhound, but now retired. He lives with his huskies, winning dog sledge races for a living.

First thing in the morning when 'what-there-is' of a sunrise, he got up to feed his dog, ate breakfast then went out to prepare his sledge for the race.

Once at the race track he attached his dogs to the sledge and soon enough the race started. The grinding noise of the sledges can be heard for miles. Lap one, lap two, lap three, the laps passed one by one.

'So far, so good,' said Snake but then suddenly a wire snapped and a dog runs onto the left. Crack, the sledge slips and the dog lies on the ground.

'Nooo!' screamed Snake running towards the wounded dog. It was still breathing . . . still alive. Snake jumped in the sledge, got to the vets and placed the dog on the counter and screamed 'Help my huskie!' not bothering to finish the race.

Later he went back to pick up the injured dog, took it home, fed it and put it to bed.

'Oh well,' he sighed before going to bed, 'I guess I can't win them all.'

Michael Hanns (12)
Glenburn Primary School

The Day In The Life Of Ginger

It is 7.00pm in the evening, this is when I get up, around when it starts to get dark. I'm called Ginger. I have a browny-orange coat and black eyes.

I don't do much. My owner has to think about lots of things, but me, I only need to think about a couple of things like my wheel and food. I don't have to think about school or having to get up early in the morning.

I live here in my cage and it's very cosy too at 24 Carrick Street, Maybole.

I'm away to have a run now, why don't you come with me?

I . . . love . . . having . . . a little . . . run. Yeah! It's food time, my owner gives me the best stuff ever, but her parents give me the yucky stuff. Thank goodness it's the good food.

'M'll must mo mup moo my mouse.' I just said 'I'll just go up to my house.' You see, I don't eat it from my bowl, I carry it up to my house to eat it later. I have very sharp front teeth, about a centimetre long.

It's nearly morning so I'd better get off to bed, nighty-night!

Deborah Keir (11)
Glenburn Primary School

A Day In The Life Of My Dad

One day Dad got ready to leave in his truck. He said goodbye to Mum, Liam, Kieran and I. He went out of the door and hopped in the cab. He looked down to me and said 'You're the man of the house while I'm gone so be good.' Then he left.

Dad drove along the road and after two hours he got to his first stop (Bardon Hill Quarry). He jumped out of the cab and handed in his paperwork, founds out where he should be tipping, and tips. While he is tipping he phones his boss to see where he is loading next. He finds out, leaves Bardon Hill and goes to where he has been sent. He is going to go to Scares Open Cast Coal Mine for a load of coal.

After one hour's worth of driving he gets there. Once there, he gets his paperwork and drives under the hopper. When loaded he finds out there are no other loads available today, so he tips his load and parks up for the night at Garston Docks. When parked he watches TV and reads a book. That is a day in the life of my dad.

Christopher Rae (10)
Glenluce Primary School

A Day In The Life Of My Dad

My dad tries his hardest to make sure that his family is okay. It's a difficult job. He wakes up at six o'clock and gets himself dressed, ready for a nice sunny day. He wakes my big sister, Annmarie, and then he gets my little brother up and finally he wakes me and my sister Emma.

My dad goes to the kitchen to get a cup of coffee for my mum and himself, then he goes out onto the hammock. He puts suncream on, of course, but he still comes in the house looking like a lobster.

It is now half past twelve, time for dinner. 'Mmm!' he says to himself. 'What shall I have today, beans on toast? Okay,' so he cooks beans on toast for us all. It is very nice. My dad's finished his dinner and it's now time to walk our hairy dog Max.

It's time for tea, we all have macaroni cheese. 'Mmm!' Dad says again. By now it's about half past four and my dad takes Liam and me to the park to play rugby for a while. We play until six o'clock. My dad watches a programme on the television until seven o'clock.

It's now time for bed. We all brush our teeth and my dad says 'Goodnight.' Just before that he kisses my mum goodnight and goes to bed.

Sarah McClements (10)
Guardbridge Primary School

A Day In The Life Of Myself

It is seven o'clock in the morning. The alarm clock has gone off, time to go to school. I must get up. I am getting ready. I have cornflakes for breakfast.

Time to go to school. I will be late because it is eight forty-five in the morning and I still need to get my bike out for Cycling Proficiency. My bike is pink with blue writing on. I can't find my helmet, it is green and pink with a black strap on it. Oh look, I have found it now. I have to put it on and close the shed and put the key back.

It is eight-fifty in the morning and I must cycle quickly or I will be late for school.

'Brrring, brrring.' The teacher says 'Get your maths out and do it please.' I have finished my maths and suddenly the electricity goes off. We are all sent home so there is no school for the rest of the day.

I cycle home for lunch. I have a sandwich with peanut butter. I go to my bedroom. My mum comes in and says 'What are you doing here?'
I say, 'The electricity has gone off.'
'Ooh!' says my mum.
'OK,' I say.

Leanne Chalmers (11)
Guardbridge Primary School

Day In The Life Of An Alien!

Once upon a time up in space, Freakozoid, who was an alien, got up. He always looked like a monkey when he woke up. He went back to bed half an hour later. When he woke up again at 8.00am he looked as if he was as handsome as the best looking man in the history of aliens. His room mates thought he was a movie alien.

At 12.00pm he went shopping. He felt great. For the first time in his life people looked at him in a nice way.

Later on, an old lady came over asking for a kiss but Freakozoid ran as if he was going to win the Olympics.

By 1.00pm he almost got into his UFO when the movie alien, Jennifer Lovez, came over. She thought he was beautiful. She was the prettiest of all the ladies. She took Freakozoid back to her mansion. He stayed for a while. They were in love, they adored each other.

Jennifer lived with her dad. His name was Crie. Freakozoid stayed for dinner. All Crie would do is talk. He hardly touched his food. 'Bla bla bla bla.' The couple left early for the UFO eclipse. They left in Jennifer's limo. It was 11.00pm.

Something has happened to Freakozoid.

'Ahhhhhh!' Jennifer cried. 'A monkey! Who are you? Help! Help! Helppppp!'

Colin Reid (11)
Guardbridge Primary School

A Day In The Life Of A Blue Tit

It was six in the morning. Suddenly a blue tit came to the bird feeder which was full, but when the blue tit went away it was empty.

The blue tit went down the garden to get worms so she could feed her babies. She got two worms and two beetles to feed one girl chick and one boy chick. She had twins as well, which were girls. The worms were for the twins and the beetles were for the others.

The blue tit flew through the sky. She saw a sparrow, robin, pigeon and a crow. On the way back she saw a plane. She flew down to get more food and saw lots of cars, lorries and bikes. She saw some food and went to get some for herself.

When she got back she saw a male blue tit heading towards the nest. She flew back to her nest as fast as she could. She just about hit the tree. When she got there she found out that he was the chicks' dad.

Then she noticed that the sun was going down, so she got everyone in the nest to go to sleep.

Kimberley Paterson (10)
Guardbridge Primary School

A Day In The Life Of God

God is maker of people and the world. He lives in Heaven but every day there are problems.

One pleasant, sunny morning God awoke from his soft, fluffy, cosy bed and looked out of his window. The clouds were gathering with furious anger. 'Something bad is going to happen today, someone will die and I have to make the tough decision whether they should go to Heaven or Hell.'

It's lunch time, I need to pick up my food. Every day I can have anything I want. It's actually rather boring now, but never mind. Well I'm going to have grapes with lime juice. 'Maids,' God called, 'bring me grapes with lime juice.' The grapes were bitter with anger, another sign of death.

'Ding ding,' the bells rang. A poor soul, I must go and see who it is .

'Who are you?' said God. It is a poor little girl. She had a letter, it said that this girl was run down by a roaring car but she has done many bad deeds! I think we will put her in the circle of belief *'Ping!'* - the circle appeared. The girl walked into it. Would it land on an angel or devil?

Ding, ding! Angel! The child can stay and that is life for me every day.

Beth Moffat (11)
Guardbridge Primary School

A Day In The Life Of Myself

My name is Julie and this is a story of myself. I hope you like it.

10.30 on a Saturday morning. I just want to go back to sleep but I have to get up because we are going to Dundee to spend our money.

I get up and now I have to pick some clothes to wear - jeans, T-shirt, pants, socks and a jersey, just in case. I have my breakfast, Frosties, yum yum, crunch, crunch, ooh yuck a rotten one, just as well I saw that.

'Get a move on,' shouts my mum from the living room. I brush my teeth and my hair and off we go in the car.

We are going over the Tay Bridge and we see a train crossing the railway bridge, a very long one as well. We get to the Overgate and we park the car. We get out and lock the car. We get in a lift to go to the shopping centre. We are on level two when all of a sudden the lift breaks down.
I shout 'Mum, where are you?' I was scared.
A lady picks up the emergency phone and says, 'Hello, can we have someone to fix the lift?'
The man on the other end says, 'What level are you on?'
'Level two,' she says.
'OK ma'am, we'll be right there.'

They are there like a flash of lightning. Click, clack, turn. 'Finished, that should do the trick,' he says and it works.
My mum says, 'Let's go home,' and we do.

Julie Chalmers (9)
Guardbridge Primary School

The Owl And The Mouse

As I soared through the sky, I was looking at the stars which shone like fireflies in the sky. I was hunting after a day's rest so that I could feed the owlets that were in the old barn, although right now they look like tiny balls of fluff.

Then I saw a flash of grey amongst the grass. I swooped down and caught the mouse between my claws.

'Please don't hurt me?' begged the mouse. 'You'll be grateful!'
'All right,' I said, 'but I'd better be.'

Well I suppose I'd better get home, I thought crossly for I was very hungry. Suddenly I heard a tearing noise and blood splattered all over my wing. I turned around to see what it was. I was caught in barbed wire! What if I lost too much blood? What would happen to the owlets? I felt sick with fear. I called in a desperate voice 'Mouse!'

It seemed like hours until I heard the reply. At last mouse appeared with his family and they gnawed at the wire until I was free. They wrapped some grass around my wing. After that I thanked them and flew (with some difficulty) home.

The owlets were petrified. I should have been back hours ago! They hooted with joy when they saw me. I told them what had happened and warned them never to kill a mouse because even if it's the smallest creature it could be the biggest help.

Rebecca Darge (10)
Hermitage Park Primary School

A Dog's Day

It's Wednesday today, a normal day for me. It all started when I, Rascal Cranston, was sitting in my bed, the basket, under the stairs. I saw the door open. My mum was there, she had opened the back door too. I walked outside to my toilet area. After that I just went back to bed. An hour later I saw Andrew opening the door, bellowing 'Rascal!' I jumped out of bed, ran through. Time for my breakfast - dog meat and biscuits. Then I saw my escape to freedom by following Andrew. I jumped past Dad making my water bowl fall over him.

'Bad, stupid dog!' he yelled at the top of his voice.

I zoomed past Gavin while he shouted 'Rascal come back.' My paws were soaking wet making paw marks. They were following me but I was faster. I fell into mud, I shook most of it off but some was still on me. Then I ran right up to Andrew who said loudly 'Rascal!'

Next thing I knew I was in my bed waiting for my family to come back. About five hours later my mum came back. She let me out then went to eat a biscuit, but before she could I grabbed it and ate it. 'Bad, bad boy!' Mum said. I was upset and was put back to my bed. Later Gavin and Andrew came in. Gavin opened the door and I raced out of the stairs and I ran to Andrew, who was all wet from the rain. He clapped me and said 'Good, good boy.' Then after my family's tea they took me for a walk in the park, far away. They put me in the boot of the car and they drove away. Later in the car I felt strange and I was sick.

It was everywhere. Yuck, mess, I was in deep trouble. I was locked in my cupboard. What an end to my day.

Andrew Cranston (10)
Hermitage Park Primary School

A Day In The Life Of A Cat

My name is Liam. I am a cat. I am brown and black. Usually I get up at about eight. The humans have left the house and I'm hungry. The humans have left some food out for me and some milk.

I decide to go out after I have slept for a few hours. Yawn! That was a good sleep I've had. I decide to go into master David's room, although I'm scared of his bed because it is on poles holding it up.

Now it is time for the humans to come home. They will sit in front of the magic box and I go out for a bit where I meet my friends. Smudge likes to bully other cats especially one called Dave, a black and white cat. There is a sudden fight between Dave and Smudge. I just run from it. Usually I never leave my street but tonight I feel I want adventure so I go three streets away where the cats are like lions. I am really scared. I see a dog the size of a table. I run for it, then I'm in the window and on my owner's lap, safe at last.

David Osler (11)
Hermitage Park Primary School

A Day With Norman And His New Owner

Hi, I'm Norman. I'm a dog and have one brother but I don't know where he is. I lost him when I was taken into the cat and dog home.

One day when I was sleeping in my kennel I heard that Mr and Mrs Bernard came over from America. The next thing I knew I was in the back of a large car on the motorway. Mr Bernard stopped in front of a tan coloured hotel which towered over me. I was carried out of the car by Mrs Bernard who was small, fat and she wore bright red lipstick. I stayed with my new owners in the hotel for another week and then we flew back to America in their very own jet.

I was amazed with this jet, I'd never been in one like it and I got to run about in the back and play with Mrs Bernard. 'Oh I'm so glad we chose you, Norm,' said Mrs Bernard. It felt weird when she said that so I just continued to play around. Mr Bernard landed on a runway which had grass on each side of it and it didn't look like an airport. There was only one runway and nothing else. He taxied into a small hanger which had a car in the front of it. Mr Bernard opened the door and lifted me out, he unlocked another door that led to their house. Their house was massive. I even had a room!

Craig Smith (11)
Hermitage Park Primary School

A Day In The Life Of A Hamster

I'm a hamster called Roman but my human family all call me Romy. Today is boiling, the sun won't hide behind any clouds, it just wants to stay out so everyone can see it.

My family are in the living room watching TV and I'm playing on my wheel. I thought because nobody was playing with me, I wanted to escape so I did. I squeezed myself through a gap in my cage and I was soon down the street. A tabby cat saw me and chased after me until I fell down the drain and landed on a piece of square sponge. It took me away down a hole and soon came out the other side to find huge, well detailed buildings standing in rows of three. Cars went zooming past me every two seconds and nearly ran me over because I was off the kerb. I made my way across the road with a lot of hassle and after a while, I finally realised that I must have been in some sort of town. My feet started to hurt as I walked along a cobbled stone path and before I knew it, I came to a dark and dusty hole. When I went in I met a mouse and he gave me food and water. I was free and this was the best day ever and this was how I lived for the rest of my life.

Connor Wood (10)
Hermitage Park Primary School

A Day In The Life Of A Page Boy

My name is Harry and today it is the fifteenth of December 1251. I have just woken up very early. My first task is to put the Lord's clothes on his bed and then I will go to see if breakfast is ready. It was, so I served it to the Lord and Lady, it is ale and bread today.

The Lord, or Uncle Hedrick, said he'd go out hunting with his squires and for a special treat, or an early birthday present, I could go. The only bad thing is my brother Henry's a squire, unfortunately he had to come too.

When I went out it was really cold. The Lord helped me up on Henry's horse. It was fun watching the dogs run really fast. The woods were dark and Henry's horse was trotting beside the Lord. I started to daydream about my ninth birthday, Henry will be sixteen in April.

Unfortunately I did not see a low branch, I fell off Henry's horse and it was sore. The Lord took me back to his castle. He said I should practise some archery. The Lord put a circle on the trunk of a tree. I held the bow and arrow, lined it up and fixed it. Just as the Lord turned round it hit the target right in the middle, I felt very happy. The Lord was pleased and I proudly went to bed.

Samantha Drummond (9)
Inverkeithing Primary School

A Day In The Life Of A Puppy

It was a Sunday morning and I was sleeping in my bed. The birds were singing and they woke me up. I went through to the kitchen. I went to my food bowl, then I saw the back door open. I walked over and looked outside, a breeze of wind went by. Then I popped my head back in.

I started to walk outside. My owner was out the front. I walked over to a ball and started to bite it. I walked about the garden, I saw toys on the ground. I saw a cat on a wall licking itself. I barked at it and the cat ran onto another wall. I started to walk down the driveway, cars were going past. I saw children playing football and tig. I started to walk forward and my owner saw me and she put me in the house.

It was late at night, my owner sat down in her chair to watch TV. Before my owner went to bed I got my supper and then I went to my bed and I fell asleep.

Liam Graham (9)
Inverkeithing Primary School

A Day In The Life Of A Page

I woke up this morning and felt excited. I went to the solar and got the Lord ready for tournament. After that we set off to Birmingham for the tournament.

The first to take part was Big Bully Ben against Arthur the Amazing. Next was Sir Tomhas the Terrible against William the Walloper. The final was Arthur the Amazing against Sir Tomhas the Terrible. The winner was Arthur the Amazing. Sir Tomhas the Terrible's helmet had to get taken off by the blacksmith. I said to myself 'What a fair and fun tournament!' I got home and said to myself 'What a fun and exciting afternoon I've had.'

After that Frederick and I practised some archery, it was great fun. After that it was about dinner time and I had to serve the Lord. Then I went hunting for the first time. We had to hunt wild boars. It took quite a long time to catch one and it was really dangerous as well. I had a great time. We got home, I went to bed after I had some water and bread. It was a fun day. I enjoyed the tournament at the start of the day and I liked the hunting as well as the archery.

Danny Lamond (9)
Inverkeithing Primary School

A Day In The Life Of A Servant

I'm Elizabeth Wallace, a Saxon servant from the south of England. I'm twenty-four years old. It's 1262 on a cold morning. It wasn't just any kind of day, it was Christmas.

One of my chores is to set out the Lady's clothes but I forgot. I didn't mean to and I said I was very sorry, but my Lady boxed my ears for me.

Everyone was excited because it was Christmas and the jesters were coming in the evening. My friend Mary and I were hanging up decorations when we saw the Lord coming, so Mary opened the door for him. He was with the new page, his name was Harry. I brought Lady Olivia some food and I told Harry how to serve it. The Lady had bread, wine and fish, the page had to serve it. I went to clean the Lady's clothes.

That night because we had guests we had a huge meal with chicken, bread, carrots, rabbit, pig, potatoes, boar's head and peacock. The guests also had wine, ale and water.

After the meal the jesters came. They did tricks and some people were playing music. Some acrobats came and did special tricks like flips, turns, jumps and cartwheels.

Harry got a colourful feather from his Uncle Harrold from a castle in London. Soon it was time for bed. Mary and I had to blow all the candles out and then we went to bed.

Lorraine Johnstone (9)
Inverkeithing Primary School

A Day In The Life Of A Puppy

My name is Sparky. I am three months old and I am black. I live with my boy Tom and his mum and dad.

One day I was sitting on my boy's bed. I woke up and I saw that the back door was open. Nothing like this had ever happened to me before. I tiptoed down the stairs. I looked left and right to see if someone was there but there was only me. I poked my head out and I jumped. There was something out there that burnt my nose. I went back out and I sniffed the air, it was fresh. I went over to this thing that had a scent of a fresh bone. I love bones!

Whilst I was sniffing this lovely thing, all of a sudden the biggest bulldog ever jumped out from the next door neighbour's garden! I was shaking. I had never seen such a fierce look on its face. It scratched my paw, I was very angry. I charged at him with all my force and bit him.

'Ouch,' said the bulldog. The bulldog ran away. I felt so scared at first but then I felt like a hero!

Tom came home at last from school and came into the garden. He asked where I had been. He saw my paw was cut and said he would go and get some bandages. He bandaged me up and put me in my basket and that was the end of my busy day.

Dale Robson (9)
Inverkeithing Primary School

A Day In The Life Of A Puppy

My name is Millie. I am a white West Highland terrier and I am six months old. It's a Monday morning and the sun is shining. I've just woken up from my sleep. I went to get my toy and I started to play with it. I was jumping up in the air to catch it, it was fun. Then I went for my first walk, I felt really excited. We went for a long walk, there were exciting smells. After we came back I felt tired so I went for another sleep for half an hour.

Later I woke back up and I went for something to eat. I got a biscuit then I went and ate it. I got my toy and I started to play again. I love my toy. I liked jumping in the air and I also like running after it. After that I went to get my dinner. I had a drink of water and some Pedigree Chum. Later I went out in the garden to do the toilet then I came back in and got another drink of water. I went back to play. This time I went and got my ring. It went over my head and I couldn't get it off, so I went through to the kitchen and my owner got it off my head. I was barking then I went back to play. After that I went for another walk but this time it wasn't long. When we came back it was getting dark so we went to bed and the lights went off. It had been another busy day.

Lauren McBride (9)
Inverkeithing Primary School

A Day In The Life Of A Servant

It is the 8th September 1249, I am Margaret Stuart, a Saxon servant in York castle. I am 20. Just now I'm putting my hair in pigtails because my Lady doesn't like people wearing their hair all over the place and, of course, it's extremely unpleasant. Anyway, enough of that, I'd better get to work.

Today's going to be really exciting. It's the King's birthday. We're having a big celebration with acrobats and musicians. Then we're having a big feast.

It's my first month in the castle and I'm still really nervous. I saw the King and Queen but they never paid much attention. I'm just in the store room now. We keep food in these big barrels. We have to put lots of salt in with food to keep it fresh. I've got to go to the kitchen now to help cook prepare the food. The kitchen's always really busy. It's usually my job to help serve the food. Today my Lord and Lady are having wild boar, but for the feast tonight there will be many things.

Later I helped put up decorations in the great hall for the King's surprise birthday celebration.

That night we had a wonderful celebration. There were jugglers, acrobats, musicians and a jester. The jester was so funny the King started crying with laughter. We ate and sang, and Mary and I were rushed off our feet but later had some leftovers in the kitchen.

That night I was really tired, but I had had a wonderful day.

Caitlin Macmillan (9)
Inverkeithing Primary School

A Day In The Life Of A Hamster

It was Wednesday morning and I was asleep. A noise woke me up. My owner was getting ready for work. She put some food in my food bowl.

But what was this? She had left the cage door open a little bit. I climbed up my ladder and ate some of my food. I went back down my ladder, got a drink of water then climbed up my cage. I pushed the door with my head and jumped down, I was free.

I was running around the room like mad but soon I was tired and I went back in my cage. I went onto my wheel and went backwards and forwards in it. I went in my little tunnel. Later I went to sleep and my owner came home and put me in my ball and cleaned my cage. My owner put a wooden house in my cage, I went back to sleep.

Suddenly a big noise woke me up. It was my owner slamming the door. I went out of my house and up the ladder. I ate some of my food and climbed up onto the cage roof and did the monkey bars. Then I scampered down the ladder, got a drink and went in my tunnel. I went back into my little wooden house and took a drink from my drinking bottle. Just then my owner came in so I went into my little wooden house and my owner said goodnight to me.

Sean Briggs (9)
Inverkeithing Primary School

A Day In The Life Of A Kitten

One Friday I woke up and got up on all my legs. I curved my back in a semi-circle and opened my mouth and yawned. I was thinking it would be a nice sunny day outside.

I went to the door and popped my head round. It was all white! I sniffed the air and then I sniffed the white stuff. I put my paw in it and made a print in it. I put all four of my legs in it. It felt nice and I started to roll about on my back.

My owner saw me outside and told me to get out of the snow. He took me inside and got a towel and rubbed it all over my body. I enjoyed this a lot and I purred as loud as a lion.

He let me down and I walked to the living room. Then he put the fire on. I pounced on my cat bed and my eyes were getting heavier and heavier. I drifted off to sleep.

As I slept I dreamed I was in the snow but it wasn't cold at all. I was looking out at the stars, thousands upon thousands of miles away in space, glittering like little silver balls.

Ross Milton (9)
Inverkeithing Primary School

A Day In The Life Of A Kitten

I was sleeping happily in my warm, cosy bed. When the curtains opened the sun was hot on my head and my whiskers twitched. I was waking up. I stretched my paws and arched my back like my mum taught me.

I was wandering about in the hall. When I realised that the door was open I walked up to the opened door and I popped my little head out and straight back in. Something whooshed past my face. It was cold. I popped out again and went down the steps. I saw something that looked like a swimming pool. I toddled over and put my paw in. I jumped back. It was wet, I didn't like that.

Just then I saw something yellow swimming in the pool. I put my paw back in and bought it out again. It was slapping about. It slid back into the water. I tried again but with two paws but it kept on slipping into the water.

Then I saw something else. Something was on the other side of the garden, so I crept closer and finally I saw it. It was my mum. I was so happy. We rubbed our faces together. My mum licked me from head to toe and I purred.

My owner was shouting so we both ran into the house, had some milk and fell asleep, curled up in a ball.

Nicole Leighton (9)
Inverkeithing Primary School

A Day In The Life Of Mrs Dunlop

Brrring! Mrs Dunlop's alarm clock went at 7am. It was Monday morning and she had to get ready to teach her P7 class at Kinglassie Primary School. She crawled out of her bed and had a look out of the window. It was still dark but she could just make out the outline of her mini. She rubbed her eyes and walked to her wardrobe and pulled out a black dress with pink flowers all over it, and a pair of black high heels. Slowly she put them on then she went down the stairs to find that her husband had made her breakfast. She scoffed it down her throat and she went outside and climbed into her Mini. She drove off to school.

When she parked her car in the car park she saw Mrs Hodgekinson walk into the school. As she ran after her, Mrs Dunlop tripped over her heel and fell flat on her nose, she had a big cut across it. She went to the office to get a plaster but unfortunately there were only blue plasters so she looked like Mrs Dunlop the blue nosed teacher.

She walked into her classroom and found her class throwing paper aeroplanes about. They looked at her and started to laugh. Mrs Dunlop did what she would normally did whether they were good or bad. She gave them loads of maths.

Vicky Hamilton (12)
Kinglassie Primary School

A Day In The Life Of My Head Teacher

I yawned as I stretched out on my king-sized bed. 'Time to get ready for school,' I sighed. I got up and looked in the mirror. 'Aaaaaaa!' I screeched. I was standing, in the body of my head teacher. I stood looking at myself strangely for a few minutes, then a surge of power zapped through me. 'I could take over the whole school like this.'

I quickly threw my clothes on and ran outside to catch the bus. Then I saw what people thought was my car. The silver Porsche was parked in front of me begging to be driven. I ran inside, got the keys and started up the engine. *'Screeecchhh!'* The car skidded on the road - 40mph, 60mph, 100mph. I was getting faster by the minute.

Suddenly a police car pulled up beside me and I slowed down.

'Well, well Mrs Kinnaird, I never thought I would have to give you a ticket. You normally drive at 20mph.' He handed me a ticket and drove off. I couldn't help smirking to myself. Ha, ha, Mrs Kinnaird's perfect little record totally spoilt. I started the engine and drove off - even faster.

I parked in the school car park and looked around. *No cars!* 'That's strange,' I thought, 'the teachers never walk to school.' I went to the school entrance and walked in.

'Surprise!' the teachers screamed. Wow, a party for me! It must have been for Mrs Kinnaird's hard work. Excellent! I didn't even do anything. I went in and danced the day away. It was brilliant.

I thought that being a head teacher was great. But do you know what? I had only tasted the half of it . . . so far!

Hazel Hunter (11)
Kinglassie Primary School

A Day In The Life Of My Cat

As I wake up I hear my owner's voice. 'Morning Albert, geez a kissy,' he says as he gives me a kiss on the head. Then I get up and start to get my owner to follow me downstairs. He gets out of his lying machine thingy and scratches the fur on his head. 'Miaow,' I shout at the top of the stairs. He races downstairs and so do I, but I give him a head start because I'm faster than him. He disappears into my room and shuts the door on me! I sit and scream and try to open the door.

'Dinner is served,' he says and guess what? It's turkey! As usual I gobble it up in about two minutes while my owner goes upstairs back to his lying machine thingy room. He puts his extra layers of woolly fur onto his skin and his owner (who he calls Dad) tells him to get in the car with me.

'Why!' he shouts.
'Because we're taking Albert to the vet!' Dad shouts back

Dum, dum, dum! I shake my head in shock. What is a vet anyway? Before I have time to decide whether to run or not, I hear a voice. 'Come on stinky,' my owner says. I jump into the car and lie down. He strokes my back and I shiver all the way down my spine. Soon the car stops. I walk into a strange building with other cats and juicy rabbits. I am taken into a room full of bottles with different colours of water (medicine) in them. I look up at a tub with a juicy bone in it which makes my mouth water (thermometer). Then a human takes it out and 'miaow' he puts it in a place I don't want to mention. He tells my owner I'm a healthy cat and gives me back to him. I could have told you that! I think to myself as I walk out of the surgery as if I've broken both my legs.

Kristoffer Beaton (11)
Kinglassie Primary School

A DAY IN THE LIFE OF MY BARBIE

Today was just like another day in a dark, cold box with nothing to do. When I woke up I felt something tugging my hair. I peeked round and saw Ashley brushing my hair. I had got some brand new clothes on. It felt terrific! Ashley took me outside and put me in a nice comfortable seat. I heard a loud rumbling noise then we started to move. After a while we stopped. Ashley and her mum were on the way to a big building. We went up some stairs, I was scared to look down in case I fell.

I was changed once again, this time into a swimming costume. I saw some water. 'Cool,' I thought, 'maybe Ken will be here.' I fell into the water and I started to sink. I was screaming but no one heard me. Ashley jumped in after me and grabbed me. Thank goodness I was OK. I had thought I was going to drown. I was placed on the side of the pool. I saw Ashley playing in the water. It made me feel like I was in the box again watching her having fun. When she came out of the water I went and got my clothes on and went back into a comfortable seat. This time it was my car. I love driving. I got stuck into some mud and I fell out of the car and into the mud. I was wet and totally soggy. I felt really cold. 'What are you doing there?' said Ashley smiling at me. I felt loved and cared for. We got home and I was put in the Barbie home with Ken! I asked him what he had been doing all day. He told me he spent the day in James' school bag. I told him all about my adventure while we made something to eat. He told me he was happy for me but I think he was jealous.

Ashley Digan (11)
Kinglassie Primary School

A Day In The Life Of A Hamster!

Whoa! Whoa! My room shook from side to side. I could hear a really loud buzzing noise in my ear. Thud! My room hit the floor and my room door opened.

I peered out the door and I saw a really big, fierce creature. It looked a bit like my pet Emma but it was much bigger. Oh no, this had happened before, I knew what was coming next. I hid under my covers as I knew any minute now the creature would poke all my toys with a long, noisy stick and all my bedding would start flying around my room. Before long the noise stopped and my room was back up the right way.

When I decided to look again, I realised I wasn't in my room. I was standing in Emma's huge room. The noise started again and the monster was going back and forth coming towards me. I quickly rushed over to the entrance of Emma's room and turned the corner. I was standing looking down the side of an enormous mountain. Panting for breath, I scuttled over to a slippery mat with 'Starburst' written on the side of it. I pushed it over to the side of the mountain and sat down.

Weah! I was away, sliding down one cliff edge after another. When I reached the bottom I skidded to a halt. There in front of me was another owner of Emma's (Molly the cat), she is bigger than me and has great, fierce teeth. I know she doesn't like me because of the last incident we had. What could I do? I was going to get eaten. Molly had me in a corner hissing and scratching me when Emma walked in.

'Get off Molly,' she shouted kicking Molly out of the road. 'How did you get down here?' Emma scratched behind my ears and put me back in my room with an extra supply of hammy nuts.

Kayleigh Wallace (11)
Kinglassie Primary School

A DAY IN THE LIVE OF A GHOST

I glided through the town towards a building which had previously been named *Bank.* The word *Bank* had been scored out and US Ghost Federation HQ painted in.

'Welcome to Las Vegas Ghost Town. Here are the rules,' said the ghost facing me.

Rules

1. Scare more than six humans a day.

2. Don't ever leave the town.

'Yes sir,' I said to him. I left the HQ. Just then I heard the very faint sound of a car engine. I flew back and told my boss.

'This one's yours,' he ordered. I began to get excited. The strange red and silver contraption parked at the entrance to the town. Five humans began walking in the direction of the tavern.

'I have an idea,' I said to myself. I glided into the tavern, went behind the bar, collected a glass and waited for them to arrive. A moment later the group walked in.

'Hello!' a young man shouted. 'Can somebody get us a b . . .' He stopped short. I had started filling the beer glass up and to them it looked as if it was happening by itself. *Clank!* The beer glass smashed at their feet. Their faces went pure white. I felt smug and happy as I watched them run out the door. They made their way to the tin tower at the entrance of the town. My fun was not over yet.

I followed them to the tower and slowly opened the door. *Creak!* I looked at their faces and they looked as though they had just seen a ghost. The human who seemed to be in-charge of the others, stepped into the building and looked around. I began to rattle the window frame and she ran out screaming. The rest of the humans followed her. They all clambered into the car and took off at great speed. I burst out laughing and thought to myself 'Not bad for my first day's work.'

Gary Harding (11)
Kinglassie Primary School

A Night In The Death Of A Ghost

'It's a full moon.'
'Yeaarrggh!'
'Ha, ha, ha.'
'Owwww!'
'That got 'em,' cackled a voice.
Three spooky shadows emerged from the darkness.
'Look at her run!' said one of the three *ghosts!*
They were unusually dressed. One had an eerie souwester and a beard, the other had an army helmet and uniform and the last, braces and big glasses.
'Wanna go clubbin'?' suggested the army ghost.
'I agree with Sergeant Spooks,' said the cowboy ghost.
'So do I!' said the geeky ghost.
'Alright, so Billy the Undead and DataBase agree' eagerly said the sergeant. 'Let's go!'
The ghost started to float down into town.
'You can't come in here!' argued the bouncer. 'We're full up!'
Just then the three ghosts came round the corner.
'You lot can't co . . . *Yikes ghosts!* I'm outa here!' yelled the bouncer.
'Ha, ha,' snorted Billy the Undead.
The ghosts floated into the club, it was so busy no one noticed them.
'Cool!' commented DataBase.
'Let's go get a drink,' suggested the sergeant. As they floated to the bar they saw numerous gobsmacked people.
'Three cans of Irn Bru,' ordered DataBase.
'Yikes, gggghosts,' said the bartender fainting and knocking on the fire alarm.
'Just as well we didn't bring Cinderella, she'd melt!' said Billy.
'Let's scare people while we still have a chance' rushed the sergeant.
Just then three voices said, 'Going somewhere?'
It was three lady ghosts. Later on the ghosts headed back to their haunted house but 'Oh no, it's daytime!'

Lewis Mackenzie (11)
Kirklandpark Primary School

A Day In The Life Of Alex On The Wall

Hello, I'm Alex I have a wife and two kids. Today as usual I'm going to get the food and money. I think I'll fly today it's easier than getting the bus. Oh, sorry, did I forget to tell you? I'm a fly! Now, work's about 20 minutes from here so I'll meet you there.

Hi again, now we're at work I must tell you something, my boss he's a . . . spider! So be careful, one wrong move and you'll be lunch, tea and breakfast. Well the work bit is a mega bore so we'll miss this part.

Next on the agenda is getting food. There's a great place just down the road. Right, we're here and now we will wait. An hour or five later and we're in, now to the kitchen. Oh look a furry thing. Right, I'll have a slice of bread and a crisp, that will do. Aahh! Humans. Oh no, two of them, hide Alex hide, just stay still.
'Yes the bomb is at the station.' Oh my God. I have to do something, the human is going to blow up the train station!

I dropped my shopping and flew as fast as I could out of the door and to the train station but I couldn't see a bomb anywhere. I slumped myself helplessly on a bench and then I heard a ticking noise. I looked under the bench and there was a bomb. Suddenly I knew all about detonating bombs. I saved the day and became famous. So I guess you could say it was an extraordinary day for Alex on the wall.

Hollie Broadbent (11)
Kirklandpark Primary School

A DAY IN THE LIFE OF A SPIDER

I lay in bed, tossing and turning, going over the day in my head and getting madder as I did. I had had a lousy day from beginning to end, everything had gone wrong. My eyes wandered to the spider on my wall, and I thought, 'Wouldn't it be great to be that spider, just for one day, please Lord, oh please Lord,' I wished and slowly drifted off to sleep.

When I woke up I found myself clinging to the wall, I let out a scream and fell to the ground, bouncing as I hit the floor. I looked round shocked until I caught my reflection in a tiny piece of shattered glass.
'Aaaahhh,' I screamed because suddenly I was a spider!
Slightly confused but nonetheless happy I scrambled out of the bedroom to the top of the stairs and hurried down them into the kitchen where I climbed up onto a work surface and tucked into a dead fly that was just lying there when, 'Aaahhh! Help Mam it's a spider! Oh help Mam!' screeched Lara. I noticed she was wearing her school jumper and had ravioli slopped down it, it must be four o'clock!
'Oh quit being such a wimp,' said Tom scooping me up in his hands. 'It's just a stupid spider.'
'No, no, no,' I screamed, and then reminded myself I was a spider and he couldn't hear me. He charged up the stairs and quietly tiptoed into my room and stuck me in my bed.
'Ha, ha, ha, she won't like that, will she?' he whispered.
Slowly I fell asleep and went to school next day as a human!

Sarah Wood (11)
Kirklandpark Primary School

POLLY THE PARROT

'Ahhh,' thud, oh there goes another couple of my feathers. Soon I will have none left. Oh hello. I am Polly the parrot. I am always bashing into things. If you think I haven't got a home, I have but sometimes I fly out of my cage and outside. And I like listening in to people's chats because that means I can pass it over to my friends. I do it every day and tease the cat and eat some crackers - they're my favourite!

Every Monday and Thursday I have to go to the vet's because I lose so many feathers, but Friday to Sunday are good, relaxing days for me. My owner tries to teach me how to talk and I don't because it's my day off from work.
'Polly! Crackers!'
Squawk, better go! Oh crackers, my lovely crackers.

Stephanie Stuart (12)
Kirklandpark Primary School

A Day In The Life Of A Chimney Sweep

As soon as I woke up on the park bench I went straight to work. I work as a chimney sweep and it's my job to go to everyone's house and clean their chimneys.

On my way to work I had a little rummage in a few bins to find breakfast. When I got to work I got a list of houses I had to go to. The list had all the same house numbers I had been doing for years but then I noticed a new house number it was 108 Long Leave Road. Long Leave Road is a very posh road, as all the big houses are there!

I worked hard all day up and down ladders, in and out of houses and at last I was finished. Then I remembered about the big house. I went and knocked on the door, a lady let me in. She looked upset but I didn't say anything.

I got started, first I had to go up on the roof. When I was climbing back down I saw something glittering in the gutter. I went to see what it was. It was a ring!
'A ring!' I shouted.

It was a ring with a big diamond on it. I took it to the lady, she was so happy. She had lost it and was worried about it.

She said that she would do anything for me. I asked her if I could get something to eat. She gave me something to eat but not only that she adopted me. *I was so happy!*

That was the best day of my life.

Louise Mackenzie (11)
Kirklandpark Primary School

A Day In The Life Of A Beetle

As soon as I got out of bed, I could hear people talking. Hi, my name is Arnold and I am a beetle. I live in the city under one of the houses. The people who live in the house are very noisy. There are three children that live in the house and I can always hear them arguing.

I am always going outside just for a walk and something always goes wrong, although today is a lovely day for a walk. I think I'll go for a walk today.

I was ready now for my walk, so I left my house. I had brought some of my money with me so I could buy something.

'Aaaah,' I cried. I had fallen over when I was walking along the pavement and dropped all my money. I started to chase after it, it rolled down all the streets. I was beginning to get very tired because I had to run around half the city trying to catch my money. I had just caught my money when someone bumped into me and I dropped it again but this time it fell down a drain. I jumped down the drain, got my money and got out another drain that was right next to my house.I climbed into my bed. I was asleep after about two minutes.

Katie Duffus (11)
Kirklandpark Primary School

A Day In The Life Of A House Mouse

'Yikes,' I thought as the rear end of my body skidded round the corner, the hideous monster still at my tail. 'Nice kitty, you really don't want to eat me,' I mumbled as the mouse-eating creature came towards me. I was trapped. This was it, I was going to die, a horrible, painful death. Then a sudden idea came to my small but clever brain. I dashed between the cat's legs quicker than I could say mouse-for-tea. I ran until I got back to my cosy hole in the wall. I trudged over to my matchbox bed and snuggled down under my blanket. I thought how lucky I was to be alive!

I woke up to a lovely smell. 'Mmm, I'm hungry,' I said remembering I didn't have tea last night. My stomach soon got the better of me. I found myself walking out my hole and looking cautiously around the vast room for any signs of the monster.

When I was in the kitchen, smoke was rising out of a frying pan. 'Yum, yum, mushrooms!' I crept up the cupboard and along the shiny surface. At last I was there but not for long.
'Aaaggghhh,' shrieked Mrs Smith's terrified voice. 'That mouse again!' I jumped off the smooth surface, forgetting what I heard last night (Mrs Smith was setting traps). I tripped over the table leg and was millimetres away from having my tail chopped off by a mousetrap, I had injured my paw when I landed so I hobbled as fast as I could back to my hole and went straight to bed.

Luckily my paw is fine today, but the bad news is the cat has now got three kittens!

Isla Cruickshank (11)
Kirklandpark Primary School

CHELSEA THE ORPHAN

'Roar! The lion's woken up and is heading this way.' I whispered to Caroline. 'And is not in a very good mood.'
'Better stand clear,' said Lucy.

Caroline, Lucy and I are all orphans from the Queen Victoria Orphanage, Bond Street, London.
By the way I'm Chelsea, I'm 11 years old and I've been an orphan since I was 2 (in 1879) so has Caroline. But anyway back to the story.

Miss Crabby (the lion/teacher) walks in so we all get out of bed and line up, and each in turn make our beds, after that we get to work. Caroline and I start getting the stairs swept then washed, it's not that hard but your arm gets sore! After that it's breakfast - yuk - lumpy, cold porridge. I don't like it so I give it to Mr Eat All (the toilet). It clogged the drains, so poor Kimmy had to clean it out, and since I didn't admit to it, we all got the belt and no supper.

After that more hard labour, Kimmy and Lucy have to do the sweeping whilst Caroline and I do our maths, then we swapped over. Caroline and I did the ironing and they did the maths. After that was over it was half-past seven so we had to go to bed. As I fell asleep I was dreading the next day.
'Oh no,' I yelled. 'Miss Crabby's singing again, aaaaaaaaaa!'

Kelly Muldoon (11)
Kirklandpark Primary School

WHY DO I GET ATTENTION?

In two hours time I will be going on tour in Los Angeles. It is always the same routine, everyone goes mad and asks for my autograph. I hate getting attention, sometimes I wish I was not a pop star. It's bad enough having to move home from Glasgow to Hollywood. I mean what is wrong with Glasgow? Oh I think people are shouting outside, the bus must be in Los Angeles. You're wondering why I say Los Angeles, it is because mad city people stay out in the streets all night long plus that's where I am playing tonight at the biggest stadium in town. I am not nervous at all, well maybe a wee bit.

Oh well, it is time to get out. I had better get out of the bus. If I make a dash for it no one will see me. Quick. 'Go.' Okay, I am inside now and I have got to get changed. I can hear the crowd going wild already. I am going on now, I am really nervous.

It is all over now. I was great, people kept throwing flowers at me when I was finished. I do not know, getting attention is alright but I suppose sometime I've got to give up my singing career because I am afraid about not being popular enough. So I am no longer a singer.

I am happy to go back to Glasgow and see my friends and family again. Well, I am in Glasgow now and it is my birthday, the 21st of September. I am going to have a disco with all my friends and I have a big cake with my face on it as a singer.

Jane Hall (10)
Kirklandpark Primary School

SAMMY'S BIG ADVENTURE

'Hi, my name is Sammy and I'm a greyhound. I am five years old and -.'

'Sammy, get up now!' Bellowed a voice.

'And that's my owner, Michael Black.'

'Sammy, come and get some tasty sardines,' said Michael.

'Mmmmm. Nice. After this (don't tell Michael) we'll go out for an adventure. But first we've got to dodge a bath. This should be easy just as long as Michael doesn't notice me acting a little strange.

Right, finished. Now let's get going here and here and here. Finished, climb out of the window and I'm outside.

I think first of all I will chase a cat (just to get warmed up.) Yes! Hit the jackpot. There's that little pain of a cat next door. Creep up silently and pounce. Oh no! I missed and that's the only slow cat in the neighbourhood. Oh well, I suppose I'll just not need to warm up and just go on an adventure straight away.

What can I do? Aha. I will try and sneak into the baker's shop and steal a cake or two (the baker really doesn't like me). He won't let any dogs into his shop because he thinks we're *mangy*! I've never heard a bigger load of rubbish ever. I'll show him.

Not too far to go now, just at the end of the street. I'm there now. I can try my master plan. Just need to wait for someone to open the door. Ahhh, here's a person now who (hopefully) will go into the baker's.

Yes, I'm in. Now easy does it. Sneak past everyone's legs, behind the counter. Ahhhh. Phew, I almost blew my cover as secret agent Sammy. Ohhh. Lovely cream cakes. One of those and a pastry. Right, off I go and I don't care if I bang into people now because I am just going to start running.

There, safely home and eating my prizes.'

Neil Cameron (11)
Kirklandpark Primary School

The Big Boom

One morning a massive *boom* woke me up, immediately I knew it was the gardener again. I have had a nickname for him for ages. It's Chop Tail Ted. Ted got that name because he used to chop off all the tails of every worm he found, even the small, baby ones.

I thought nothing of the boom at first until it came again, *boom, boom, boom!* It was getting closer and closer. I ran to wake my dad up then it came again, *boom, boom!* I went as fast as I could. When he got up we ran and ran, it was still coming only faster and faster. My dad stopped for a rest, I was shouting at him to hurry up but he was just so tired. Then it came again, *boom, boom, boom!* When I looked back he was gone.
'Help, help me son!' The gardener had got him in his shovel. I stood there and watched the gardener kill him with his shovel. It was horrible, I kept running and running. I stayed under a tree for a couple of days just thinking about what had happened to my dad. I didn't want to go home but I knew I had to sooner or later.

I went back home thinking I was going to find something horrible but it was wonderful. There were tulips, lilies and roses, everything was there. It was the most glorious thing I've ever seen in my life. It felt like paradise. This place where I had lived all my life felt like paradise. I loved it so much, it was wonderful.

The flowers kept on growing all through the year. There have even been other worms that have come to live with me.

Jennifer Blair (11)
Kirklandpark Primary School

A Day In The Life Of A Honey Bee

I awoke to find my best friend Victor shaking me.
'Come on! The Queen wants honey!' he said.
'Can't the Queen wait a few more hours?' I grumbled.

Victor pulled me out of my bed of leaves and together we stumbled out of the hive and into the daylight. It was a beautiful day. The sky was clear and the grass was lush green. I began to look for some food. I eventually had a feast of pollen with Victor. Then we both went off to find nectar for the Queen.

I flew around the garden, till I found a cluster of big poppies. I filled myself up with nectar to my heart's content and then I started back to the hive.

I hadn't gone more than half-way when a child came running into the garden.
'Argh! A bee!' she cried, swatting me with her hands. Well, I wasn't standing for any of this nonsense! I grabbed onto her neck and stung her hard. She screamed, and then ran back up to her house, crying. Phew! Thank goodness that was over.

I was just about to fly into the hive, when another unwelcome visitor greeted me. A black dog came trotting down the path, its tongue lolling out of its mouth. Then it began chasing after me! It ran, I flew, but the dog was getting closer, closer . . . *clamp*. The dog's jaws closed over me. I began stinging its mouth, but it wouldn't drop me! Then he swallowed . . .

I'm sure I'll have many more adventures one day - in the dog's mouth!

Gillian Montgomery (11)
Kirklandpark Primary School

DEE DEE'S DAY OUT

I am a Yorkshire terrier called Dee Dee (my owner Mrs Winters gave me that name). Just now I am lying in my basket dreaming about today's exciting adventures. Here's what happened . . .

I opened one eye drowsily, stretched my legs, then stood up. My basket is in the kitchen so I jumped and scrambled up onto the kitchen counter and ran to the bread bin. I opened it with my teeth and scoffed every scrap of bread (I was quite hungry!). Then I skilfully unlocked the window latch and in a flash I was in the outside world. So many sights and sounds and smells, I was in a daze. But there was work to do. Oh no, a big, slobbering mutt. Run! In here, sshh . . .

Phew, I escaped within an inch of my life. I think I'll go to the park. So I went. The see-saw is my favourite thing. I like walking up and then sliding down (I'm not heavy enough to make it tilt). I had great fun at the park that day!

Mmm, I smell *ham!* (which is my favourite food in the whole universe!), so I followed the scent until I came to a man on a bench. First I grabbed a one pound note from his trouser pocket (I am an accomplished pick-pocket). Then I grabbed his ham sandwich and ran to the nearest bus stop to catch the 2 o'clock bus that would drop me at the bus stop beside my house. Then the bus came, oh good, I thought. So I got on, dropped my money at the driver's feet, jumped up on the seat and contentedly munched my sandwich. Soon it was my stop so I got out and scratched on my door. Mrs Winters took me in, put me in my basket and I lay exhausted after my exciting day. And that's where I am now.

Alan Montgomery (11)
Kirklandpark Primary School

A Day In The Life Of An Adult

Hi, I'm Annie Parker. I'm eleven and I live in a huge house in California with my dad. My mum and he separated when I was young. Last month my dad met Alison (she is his new sort of girlfriend). I absolutely hate her though I have to be nice when Dad is around. I call her Cruella. Anyway, it feels good to be myself again. What I mean by that is, well, something happened two weeks ago. I went to my bed that night really angry with Alison because she said she was going to marry Dad. I think she is only doing it for Dad's money. I wished that we could swap places to see how she liked to be hurt. I couldn't believe it when it actually happened. I woke up in the morning lying in a double bed. It was me but in Alison's body. I made such a mess of being Alison and Dad didn't know what had gotten into me as well as Alison. I jumped into the pool and splashed everything. I also wanted to do lots more stuff like go roller blading, skateboarding, buy loads of sports wear (which Alison would never do). By the evening Dad was totally put off Alison and didn't want to see her again! I was really glad when I was myself again the next morning. Am I glad Alison is gone!

Lindsay Rea (11)
Kirklandpark Primary School

A Dolphin Marriage

Now I start this is no ordinary dolphin story, do you think dolphins get married? Well in this story we do, so I'll begin!

Hi, I'm a dolphin, my name is Mark, I live under the sea off the coast of Scotland. It's not very warm but it will do!

It all started when I met this other dolphin at a restaurant called The Underwater Cafe, she had dropped her shell-like purse as she was leaving so I swam after her and gave her it back. At that moment I fell in love. I didn't know her name or phone number, but luckily for me when I got back to my house, I noticed the same pretty dolphin was my next door neighbour. Yes, I thought, I could see her every day now.

An hour went past and I could not hide it any longer, eventually I asked her out and found out her name was Rachel. We went out for an hour and eventually I asked her to marry me, she said, 'Yes!'

We had our wedding the same day and went on our honeymoon and came back after 3 hours of marriage. We had twin children and called them Regan and Simon and that was the happiest day of our lives and we lived happily ever after.

Just remember this is magic so it is possible for it to happen any day.

Rachel Hughes (12)
Kirklandpark Primary School

A DAY IN THE LIFE OF A . . . TEENAGER!

The day of his 13th birthday and he turns into a . . . a . . . Kevin.

The room of an average teenager - don't go in without a gas mask! Attention! Please don't look under my bed! Here, look at this. Last week's pizza! Watch the CDs on the floor. Don't touch that! That's my collection of toe nails. Right, here is an action replay of me and what I do.

Look, here I am in bed, the bloomin' alarm clock goes off. Out of bed and down stairs. Plonk myself down and hog the TV remote. I start calling on my mum (who waits on me hand and foot). Then she comes in and whacks me with a newspaper which reminds me of my paper round. I sloppily eat my breakfast and get ready in a rush. I do my paper round, missing out number 47. (Dog eats paper boy!) I arrive at school, late. Mr McKay asks me where my homework is and I say my sister flushed it down the loo. I find myself getting a punishment. The day goes through same as always. I arrive home and start stuffing my face with crisps. My mum tells me to do my homework, but I just ignore it. I watch The Simpsons on Sky 1. Dinner is when I eat very, very sloppily. I watch more TV and have a really big fight with my sister. I get told off and whacked with lots of pillows. 11.00pm still watching TV then I hear my dad come storming in and I run upstairs and into bed.

There! You have just spent a whole day with me. Now I have to enlarge my collection of toe nails. Bye!

Fiona Wright (11)
Kirklandpark Primary School

BLACKY THE DOG

'Blacky, wake up - breakfast time,' yelled Mum.
Not another day sitting in the house on my own.
'Get out of my way, I'm late for school!'
What did I do? I didn't do anything, did I?
'Blacky, where are my shoes?'
I didn't touch them. I wish I could talk, I'd tell them.
'Bye Blacky!'
Why do I get shut in the house all the time? They must not like me! That's what it is. They don't like me.

I know what I'll do, I'll run away. I bet they won't even notice that I'm gone. How will I get out though? I have to dig a hole. This is the hardest hole I've ever had to dig. Oh I can see a bit of grass. Oh, I'm nearly there. Yes, I'm free.

It's really cool being free. I don't need them. I can live wild! Where am I? I sure am hungry out here. I could have been having my dinner by now. But it's too late now. I'm here and I'm lost. I shouldn't have run away. It was a silly idea. They will be mad at the hole I made.

Who's that man coming towards me? Let go! Help! Help! Where are you taking me? Leave my collar alone!

Mum, Dad, Susie, Rossie! What are you doing here?
'Where have you been?' exclaimed Mum.
'Let's go home Blacky.'
Oh, we're home now. What about the hole? I thought they would be angry at me but they aren't. If all the attention wasn't enough, now I get a big, juicy bone! I'll have to do this more often!

Kirsty Jamieson (11)
Kirklandpark Primary School

A Day In The Life Of A Bowling Pin

Ahh, a fresh day, but don't forget that I am a bowling pin! I usually get knocked down a lot but today I feel lucky. But just then the bowling alley opened! Then there was a big, thundering noise. Ahhh! Stampede! Which was in actual fact all the people rushing in. Oh good, they're all choosing the other lanes! I thought. Then about 5 minutes later two boys came to my lane. Rats, it's those two, said to be good boys! The first boy picks up his ball, 'Get ready chaps!' I said.

The boy threw the ball down at us but missed us totally.
'Okay back there?' I asked.
'Yeah, we're fine!' replied one of the pins.
'Here's the next ball!'
The boy rolled the ball down. Yes, he misses.
'Third time lucky guys!' I shouted excitedly.
The boys swapped over. This must be the good boy. The boy rolled down the ball. It was heading straight for us . . . Nooooo! He struck. I hate this machine! The machine picked us up and sorted us out. The boy went again and struck a further two more times. Yes! They are swapping over again. The boy missed three times and then got a strike.
'Yahoo!' said the boy.
I hate this machine that sorts us out!
After about 15 minutes, the boys went away.
'No one seems to be coming to us,' I said.
Then everybody else started to walk away.
'Why is the Bowling Alley closing?' I asked myself. 'Oh yeah, it's Wednesday, and the Bowling Alley closes early! Yippeeeeee!' I shouted happily.

Mark Simpson (11)
Kirklandpark Primary School

A Day In The Life Of Marina

'Help, help, please help me. I beg you get me out of here.'
'I'll help you,' said green-eyed Gilbert the fishing champion. Gilbert cut the net and let Marina out.
'I am free, I can smell the fresh air again, oh how can I ever repay you?'
I swam as fast as I could to see if Daphne my dolphin was still there. I got home to see she was going mad and she had turned black and white.

I calmed her down and asked who she was she said she was Daphine's sister Luna. I asked where Daphne was, she said she was looking for her and smelt her scent here.
'How long have you been looking for her?'
'6 months,' she said 'that is how long I have had her.'
'So you must be her sister.'

'Come on I know where she is. It's where your mum died and it's your mum's birthday today too.'
'There you are, I have been looking for you all over the place, I know it's your mum's birthday but tell me if you are going out somewhere.'
'Come on let's go home.'
And they lived happily ever after.

John Dempsey (11)
Kirklandpark Primary School

A Day In The Life Of A £1 Coin

I wake up and I'm nearly always somewhere different!
'Shut up! Some 5 pences are trying to sleep!'
Oh, I'm sorry for not introducing myself. I'm a £1 coin. I've had such a busy life! I am 15 years old and rusting, all the other coins are sparkling clean. Oh no! I'm being used as change now! Every morning I wake up somewhere different. This morning it was in a Spar till and tomorrow it will probably be in a smelly, leather purse.
Ahh! I hate it when people just drop me into their deep, dark pockets as if you are a piece of rubbish, you rattle about all over the place when they walk.

Today I might explore, because the pocket that I'm in right now could be quite fun. I'm really tired and my legs are always giving way now that I'm 15. So I'm going to make a bedroom in this pocket. I've got a ball of cotton wool as a mattress, a crisp packet as the frame of my bed, a Polo mint as a pillow and a Tic Tac box as a huge bedside table.

Ahhh! A hand just picked me up with a pile of rubbish (my bedroom) I'm going in the bin! No!

Ruth Duff (11)
Kirklandpark Primary School

A Day In The Life Of Brooklyn Beckham

Hello, I'm Brooklyn and I'm two years old. I'm going to tell you about my exciting day.

I woke up this morning and started crying. My television had been switched on and I saw my mummy and daddy on it. The reason I was crying was because I don't like it when people crowd my mummy and daddy. I had a lovely breakfast, then I went out to the shops with Mummy. We had to buy me some Gucci clothes for Daddy's cup presentation.

For lunch I had a bacon roll and crisps (Daddy made it - Mummy's a health freak). It was lovely. I had it at Old Trafford - that's where Daddy plays football. Mummy was out shopping at the new Armani shop!

It was soon 3 o'clock and I had to watch Daddy play football for Man Utd - they're an amazing team. Afterwards I got to go on the pitch because Daddy was getting a cup. I saw Uncle Alex (he's leaving soon), Uncle Gary, Uncle Phillip and Uncle Jaap.

Boy was that mega exciting! I'm really tired. I had a horrible tea. It was bangers and mash, which tasted yucky. Mummy said I could have a sleepover with Al and Jordan, my bestest friends.

I had a brilliant time with Al and Jordan. We played with my mini Porsche and listened to five of my CDs. Everyone says I'm very spoiled but I don't think so. I had a brilliant day.

Clare McIntyre (12)
Kirkliston Primary School

A Day In The Life Of Nick Meathook

Hi! I'm Nick Meathook and I work for the US army. I have a mum, a sister, a brother and a dog. My dad died last year, killed by some terrorists on an aeroplane.

I'll tell you about last month and the punk who tried to kill me. Well, I had just gone to visit my gran when a street punk tried to attack me. He was wearing a black leather jacket, brown trousers and some big black boots. He had lots of piercings and a metal baseball bat, which he kept hitting me with.

I went to hospital for all the cuts and bruises I had. When I got out I went looking for the guy.

Eventually I found him but when I did he was on a tram. So I ran after him, but whilst running, he was firing at me with an Uzi 9mm and a Magnum 44, which is probably why I never caught him.

I found him again at an old factory that was used for melting things. I followed him in. The room was huge but it was just like a metal spiral ramp going down pretty far. There was a big wide furnace going down the middle. He was below me firing up. He hit me twice in the thigh, so I dropped a grenade down beside him. I thought I'd killed him but no. I saw him and said 'You're toast!' I put a bullet through his head, blew off his shoulder and he fell into the furnace.

Steven Erskine (11)
Kirkliston Primary School

A Day In The Life Of Bill Gates

I woke up and remembered it was my 47th birthday. I went to have a shower and then got dressed. After that I went down in the lift to the first floor for my breakfast and then I thought about what I was going to do for the rest of the day. I decided that I would go swimming in my pool and then go fishing with my son in our private yacht.

When we got back we were starving, so I asked the cook to make us some lunch. I had salad, orange juice and birthday cake. It was huge. Since it was my birthday there was going to be a huge party.

It was great, even George W Bush came and ex president Bill Clinton. My friends got together a present for me - it was a new plane. Just what I wanted!

By half-past twelve I was really tired, so it was time for me to go to bed. Although I couldn't sleep for thinking about whether to move house, buy another mansion or invent my very own robot waiter. But that can wait till tomorrow.

Calum Horn (11)
Kirkliston Primary School

A Day In The Life Of The Queen

Knock, knock, knock.

'Breakfast your Royal Highness!' said the servant.
'What, what, where am I?'
'Are you alright in there Queeny?'
'Em, er, yes fine, my breakfast, I have a full day ahead!'
'What are you doing today your majesty?'
'You know, I don't have a clue!'
'Well, here's your weekly agenda.'
'Oh no! I have to test baby toothpaste, to give it my seal of approval.'
Yuck, the toothpaste was completely horrid but I gave my seal anyway.

Back at Buckingham.

'Are you taking the corgis for a walk?' said Prince Charles.
'No, the boys can. Speaking of which, where are Harry and William?'
'Em, oh here they are.'
'Granny, can we have . . . ?'
'What is it today boys, hhm, Wales, a Porsche, a new suit, a house?'
'Granny, give us our pocket money!' said Harry.
'Okay, pass me my purse! Here's £1 million for you each.'
'But, but . . .' said William.
'No buts today, I'm a little strapped for cash. Off you go now, shoo, shoo!'
'I'd better be off Mother, I'm taking Camilla racing, we must do lunch sometime, ta-ta!' said Prince Charles.
'Oh bother, I forgot my mum's doing the London Marathon in her wheelchair. I hope she's okay.'
'Your Majesty, afternoon tea.'
'That'll do, go away now,' said the Queen. 'Oh I feel faint, has the servant put something in this? Uggh!'

She faints.

'Where am I? Yes, I'm home, no more Queen business.'

Holly Muir (11)
Kirkliston Primary School

A Day In The Life Of A Puppy

Hi! I'm Cleo, a very excitable ten month old golden Labrador puppy. My pet humans take ages to wake up and my favourite toy, Orange Puppy (the cat), isn't allowed in my room at night. So I have to play with my other toys, like my teddy bear or food cube.

Clonk, clonk, clonk, clonk, clonk.
'Mmm, ah Cleo, maah, ooh.' (Humans talking.)
It's my humans! 'Hello, hello, hello Mummy, hello Daddy, hello sister!'
Can I have a pat, then can I go outside.
'Cleo, walkies!'
I love walkies. Out we go, we're going along the cycle path. I hope we see Tiger, he's my best friend.

My human sister's friend came. I really like her and she's great fun to play with. I wonder what we'll play today?
'Oh hello sister's friend.' Lick, lick. 'Have you got any treats for me?'
'Ashooh eese Cleo.'
Oh good I think I'm getting to play with them. They said my name!
'Oosh ba too ese rrtanoo.'
We're playing in a room on wheels with Orange Puppy. I get to lie on a sofa, eat and get lots of games. It suits me down to the ground. Mummy's come in. She's saying something.
'Oom o eves Cleo, walkies.'
Another walk, I'm so lucky. I think we're going in the car. We are, and it's Almondell. Brilliant!

Oh, the smell of rabbits and other dogs. This is a great walk. I have chased about a hundred rabbits but now it's back home to bed.

Sarah Whittaker (11)
Kirkliston Primary School

A Day In The Life Of A Sea Explorer

I am Joe. I am 30 years old and I work as a sea explorer in Australia. I look for extinct fish that have been seen by local people, such as the blue spot butterfly fish. A very mysterious fish has been spotted but it's no ordinary fish, it's half-human. I've only got a day, starting tomorrow, to prove it.

I'm preparing for the big day tomorrow. I've got to get my waterproofs and flippers ready and so on. We have only got one rule here and that is 'If you try your hardest you will succeed'.

We are off to the Great Barrier Reef, where the fish have been spotted, and would you believe it, there was a big colony of them. It was time to take action.

'Put the nets in and make sure the ropes are very tight.'

Then one of my crew members said 'We've got one, will I harpoon it?'

'Yes' I said. There was a very loud scream. Then suddenly I said 'Stop!' I felt very guilty for what I'd done because they had a family and so have we. They're just like us.

'Let the rest of them go and let's go home!'

James McGrudden (12)
Kirkliston Primary School

A Day In The Life Of Julia Roberts

Brrriingg! Please say the alarm clock's gone off early. Huuhh, I don't know if this job's really worth getting up at 6am for! Where's my script? No one could have taken it by mistake. It says 'Julia Roberts' across the front of it! Huh, I see, someone's moved it over there. Oohh, I need more than six hours sleep.

'Hey Juls.'

'Hi Hugh.'

'Right Hugh, you're behind the bookshop. Julia, you're walking in . . . 3, 2, 1.'

'Excuse me, can I help you?'

'I'm looking for books about London.'

'Cut!'

'This is going to be a long day!'

A day's work and all we've filmed is the bookshop scene! I don't believe it! I don't like this new director one bit. All he says is 'Cut, cut, cut'!

'Right Julia, we need to leave for Parkinson in ten minutes.'

'Oohh, I forgot about that.'

'Hello Julia and welcome to Parkinson. So what do you think about this new film, Notting Hill?'

'That went terribly.'

'I'm afraid I've got more bad news for you Julia.'

'What?'

'One word, *paparazzi*. We have a limo waiting for you outside. You're just going to have to make a run for it.'

'Again?'

Gee! I'm knackered. It's 11.30! I've so much stuff I've still to do! I've got to learn the next part of the script and - oohh! It looks like it's going to be another late night!

Joanna Williamson (11)
Kirkliston Primary School

A Day In The Life Of Mr Old Moonface

It all started when a pigeon sat on my window sill. He had a letter taped onto his foot. I took the little letter off the pigeon's foot. It said 'You can come to the magical Chocolate Land on the 2nd of July 1997.' The man who sent it was called Mr Old Moonface. He said that he was sending an aeroplane to come and collect me on the 2nd of July.

It is my birthday on that date. When I got to the Chocolate Land, I met Mr Old Moonface. He lived in a huge big castle. I went in the castle to stay for a month. The castle was made from chocolate. Then, a few days later Mr Old Moonface vanished, and I never saw him again. Before I forget, today I have to phone my mum, and tell her to come and move to Chocolate Land with me and my new pet pigeon called Percy. But Mum said 'You'll have to wait a few weeks because I have to get packed and move everything into the chocolate castle.'
'OK Mum, I have to go shopping anyway,' I said.
'I'll come on the 6th of August at 3pm. I will probably arrive at that time but goodbye for now.'

Tasha Lawson (11)
Kirkliston Primary School

A Day In The Life Of Santa Claus

Beep, beep, beep, beep, beep, beep!
'Santa, it's time to get up, you've slept in. It's almost 5.01am,' shouted Mrs Claus from the kitchen.
'Oh no! I was supposed to start working a whole minute ago, that's sixty seconds wasted, you silly woman,' he replied.
'Sorry, I forgot that it's always *my* fault when *you're* late and when *you* sleep in,' she snapped.
'I didn't mean it like that and please don't start,' he pleaded 'I mean, it's Christmas Eve.'
'You're a silly darling,' she laughed. 'Come on, what would you like for breakfast, eggs or bacon?'
'Both,' he said. 'But first I have to go and attend to the reindeers.'

At the stables.

Hee, hee, hee, hee, hee, hee!
'What was that?' Santa said with a mystified look.
Hee, hee, hee, hee!
'That sounds like that cheeky dwarf, Snottles. He's probably up to mischief,' he mumbled with a frown. 'Heave! This door gets stiffer every time! . . . Aaaaahhhh!'

Back home.

'Tell me what happened again,' Mrs Claus said, when Santa told her what happened.
'Well, I was walking to the stables and I heard laughter. I thought nothing of it but when I opened the stable door, lots of water fell on my head, and I know who it was,' said he.
'Who?' questioned his wife.
'*Snottles!*'

Later at the workshop

'Right, are the toys all ready?' Santa asked one of the elves.
'Yes,' he replied.
'I'm off then, see you,' and with that he drove off into the distance.

Eve Harkness (11)
Kirkliston Primary School

A Day In The Life Of Ben Adams

Hi, my name is Ben Adams from Al. When I wake up in the morning I go in the shower and then I do my hair. I have to make it perfect because I love my hair. I have my breakfast and then I have to meet the other lads to go to film our new video 'No More'. Very tiring!

During the day I am very busy. When we film the video, I hate it when everyone is around me, putting things in my hair and making sure my clothes are perfect. My day is busier than any normal person. I am always asking my boss for a day off. But oh no! That will not be happening because every day it's work, work, work.

The other band members are all good lads. Paul's the noisiest and messiest. Christian - he is the quiet one and Mark is sort of in the middle. To me they are like family.

My feelings on being a pop star. Well, sometimes I like it, when we get to go to celebrity parties and recording a single or album. But it is very tiring and hard work because the scene on the video takes a lot of effort and it is hard to remember what to do, but I like it.

Hazel Drysdale (12)
Kirkliston Primary School

A Day In The Life Of Wallace

When William Wallace was born, that was when all the fighting went on. The English bossed the Scottish like mad. William Wallace was young and he wanted to fight the English to defeat them and be Scotland's hero. Scotland's people were frightened of the English because if they didn't do what they wanted, they would be killed instantly. So every person in Scotland became the English's slaves.

William Wallace got older and his dreams were still to slaughter the English. But most of all he wanted to kill King Edward for what he was doing and had done before. Wallace had a wife who meant very much to him and Sheriff Hazelrig barged into her house and slaughtered her. Wallace decided that meant war!

Of course Wallace never had any men to fight with so he went to villages and asked men to fight, they were not soldiers, they were just ordinary men. Wallace saw Sheriff Hazelrig at a woman's door and he thought that he was going to kill her. So Wallace fought him and you'll never guess, Hazelrig was lying on the ground with blood all over him.

Wallace started war. He saw the English coming and he had an idea to get the battle over and done with. So he and his men stood on the other side of Stirling so the English would be trapped. You wouldn't believe it, the battle was won by Wallace and his brave men. Scotland the brave.

Sarah MacDonald (10)
Lynburn Primary School

A DAY IN THE LIFE OF THE SUN

On a lovely day in the hot sun, a family went to the glen to have a picnic. It was on a Sunday afternoon. They were called Amy Matthews (the mum), Scott Matthews (the dad) and Steve Matthews (the son) and their little dog called Dude. They all sat in the Renault 19 (blue) and off they went. Steve said 'Are we there yet?'

'We will be there soon,' said Amy.

Scott laid out the picnic. Steve and Dude played. Amy lay in the bright sun. They all ate and when they were finished they all lay in the burning sun. Steve said 'This is a day in the life of the sun, isn't it Mum and Dad?'

'I agree,' said Amy.

'Me as well,' said Scott.

'Woof, woof, woof,' said Dude.

'Do you want a game of football down there on the pitch Dad?'

'I suppose so son.'

'I think I will stay and sleep here, OK?'

'Sure Mum but don't run away.'

'Pass here quickly Dad.'

OK, wait there, I'm the best footballer here,' said Dad.

'Oh stop it,' said Mum.

'Woof,' said Dude. 'Woof, woof, woof.'

Later on that night it was time to go to sleep. Steve went to bed and mumbled to himself. 'A day in the life of the best sun.'

His mum gave him a gentle kiss on the cheek and said 'Goodnight.'

Dad did the same. All of a sudden Dude jumped up on the bed and fell asleep as well.

Natasha Arnott (10)
Lynburn Primary School

A Day In The Life Of Benidorm

The journey started on the plane on the way to Benidorm. We arrived at two o'clock in the morning. Next we had to get a bus to our hotel, it was called Monica Holidays. Gorgeous inside. Just as you go in there is a drinking bar and if you look straight forward you see a large, massive swimming pool. Beside the swimming pool there was another drinking bar. However there were three bubbly Jacuzzis there and I loved them. Suddenly people were talking about this theme park and I found out it was called 'Terah Metica'. So all my family went there, it was so brilliant. I jumped really high. I didn't want to go anywhere else.

There were loads and loads of supermarkets. There were libraries but I couldn't read the books because they were all in Spanish. There was this new Harry Potter book but that was in Spanish too. I couldn't understand anything. For dinner most of the food was chips. There was a little cafe for lunchtime. There was the lovely beach and this hairdresser's and that's where I got my hair plaited.

So that was my special day in Benidorm and I had a wonderful time. We returned to Glasgow and when we found the car it was frozen. We were walking slowly because it was so cold. We got home and went to bed exhausted.

Emma Sergbine (9)
Lynburn Primary School

A Day In The Life Of Alien Al

Al the alien woke up early and went down to breakfast. He heard his brother's alarm clock, it went 'cheep, cheep' and then a trapdoor opened and Sylow, his big brother fell down. They both had Sweet Os and toast. Al saw a note on the fridge, it said '7.30am breakfast, 8am feed cats, 9am school, 12noon home time, 12.30pm lunch, 12.35pm to 3pm playing and TV time, 8.30pm bed for Al, 9pm Bed for Sylow.

Al went to get dressed. He looked in the mirror and saw a slimy green alien. He put on a white robe and his gold belt. Suddenly he saw his watch - time for school! He had clingon, art, survival, break, number - then home time.

He had lunch, which was gurger and flies with spagato ketchup. Then he played Cress with the fat blue cat next door. The game was good as gold. The cat won the game, then he watched 'Sprog in Kings Hole' on the TV.

It was time for Al to hop to bed. He had just walked to the dream station when he saw Meg and Mog. Finally he was home in bed and asleep.

Callum Corke (10)
Lynburn Primary School

A Day In The Life Of An Orphan

As the sun breaks over me, I sit up and gradually become aware of my surroundings. I'm sitting on a doorstep in a large market place, in a small town in Kosovo. Two years ago my family died of malaria. It was then that I became homeless.

Thinking about my dead parents, I hobble towards the bakery, my bare feet sting whenever I step on a sharp stone. I scan the ground, hoping that somebody might have dropped a coin. Then I see something lying, buried, in the gutter, shining.

I pick it up, my heart beating fast, and wish that I could know how much it's worth. In the bakery I ask for a roll. The man stares at me suspiciously, as if he thinks that I've stolen the coin. But he gives me the roll.

As I bite into it, I walk down a dusty lane. I notice babies wrapped in newspapers, abandoned. Children, who are very thin, scuttle past me. Suddenly I realise that there are people worse off than myself.

The town's coming alive and I dodge in and out of adults and children, looking for money but finding none. After much walking I realise it's getting late. I look for a place to sleep and eventually find a sheltered doorstep.

This is my day; wandering about and looking for money. It's always the same and it gets rather boring. It makes me hungry and tired. That doesn't make any difference; it's my life.

Anne Rutherford (11)
Noblehill Primary School

A Day In The Life Of Henry VIII

Woke up and walked briskly to my wardrobe to put on my very, very, very expensive clothes. First I put on my hose (tights) and held them in place with garters and then I put on my loose silk shirt (with *very* scratchy wool). Next I pulled my doublet over my head and further down my body. My padded shoulders felt very comfortable and helped me if I had a sore shoulder. I then placed my bloody and sharp sword into its holder (it had been ages since my horrible wife, Catherine Howard, had cleaned all the guts and blood off my beloved sword). Eventually, I placed on my flat cap and admired all the jewels on my clothes by posing to my children. They all agreed that I looked tremendous, so I thanked them and left for a hard day's work ruling the whole of England.

As I stepped out of my castle I felt my tummy rumbling. At first I thought the first ever earthquake was going to come to England! I turned round and rushed back into the castle. I sat down at the king-sized table and shouted to my cook.
He rushed to my feet and said 'What would you like for breakfast Your Majesty?'
I replied 'Cheese, hens, chickens, eggs, bacon, broth, snails, nutmeg, more bacon, perch, clover, oysters, pike, eel, cloves, more bacon, capon, mutton, pigeon, salmon, porpoise broth, toadfish, catfish, partridge, goose, saffron and, to drink, beer.'
The cook said 'Is that all sire?'
And I replied 'Oh, and some more bacon.' I demolished the plateful in seconds and said to the cook 'Well done old boy, have this gold ring.' I mutter to myself 'I've got him just where I want him!'

I stepped out of the castle once again and this time there was no turning back. I walked forward and checked my schedule. I realised this was the day I was going to chop off the head of my horse-faced wife, Catherine Howard. As I climbed up the steps of the execution block I heard someone shouting 'God Save The King.' No man could resist the temptation and I turned my head and saw the most beautiful thing since sliced bacon. I walked up to her and said, 'What's your name?'
She replied 'I'm Catherine Parr, pleased to meet you.'

I asked if she would like to join me on the throne to see the big execution.
She said 'Anything for you Sire.'
So I took her hand (and hopefully her hand in marriage soon) and we sat up on the throne.
'Sir Choppemoff, please dismiss this sleazebag.' I said. He couldn't hear me properly so I went up to him, fired him and chopped off her head myself. I felt really happy once I had Catherine Howard out of my life.

I turned to Catherine Parr and asked 'Will you be my wife?' She couldn't refuse, as I still had an axe in my hand.
'Okay,' she said, although I hope you don't chop off *my* head.'
To which I replied 'I will if I need to my darling, I will if I need to!'

Callum Wilson (10)
Noblehill Primary School

A Day In The Life Of Rachel Marshall

I woke up yawning and groaning to the familiar sounds, the odd car on the road and the cupboard doors banging. I rolled over and peered at my alarm clock in the dim light. Nearly eight. Bebeep, bebeep. 'Be quiet,' I croaked and as I expected it didn't obey. I fumbled with the switch to put my alarm off. 'Day?' I asked myself. 'Monday,' myself replied. I sat quickly up in bed. 'Bank Holiday Monday, no school today,' I said.

After a hurried shower and breakfast, Dad told us he had got a licence so we were off to move some cattle. Because we live on a farm in a foot and mouth infected area, we have to disinfect our feet and cars all the time. When we had taken two lots of cattle across roads and swept, washed and disinfected both roads, we had held up eighty cars altogether!

For the rest of the day I played in the sand with my brother John (7) and Scott (5), had a game of draughts with Dad (he won) and started writing a letter to my Canadian pen-pal Tanis, which turned out to be my biggest problem that day. I sat gnawing the end of my pencil.

Dear Tanis, I wrote, I gnawed my pencil again. Eventually I told her about school and my stage dancing class.

After tea I was surprisingly tired, so I went upstairs to get washed and changed, then nestled down under my duvet with my book. I will be ready for anything tomorrow!

Rachel Marshall (9)
Noblehill Primary School

A Day In The Life Of A Cat

Miaow! Let me introduce myself, my name is Miranda. I am a tabby cat. It's eight o'clock and Lorna should be giving me some milk about now. After my milk, I think I'll go hunting.

Now I've finished my milk I'm going hunting in the fields. I think I just saw the grass move! It couldn't have been the wind, it's too nice a day. It's a mouse and I'm going to get it, I feel peckish! When I get that mouse I'll be very happy but that tom cat is in my way. Darn, he got it! Well that's lunch off the list, now I can lay in the sun and get my ears scratched, that will be nice. It will be very nice. I wonder where Oliver and Tobias are, they are my twin sons, they need their afternoon wash. Oh, there they are now!

Is my hearing correct? Did I hear the front door open and Lorna calling 'Miranda, puss puss!' If I could talk I would tell her I am not a puss puss, I am a duchess with claws and not afraid to use them! I think I will go back inside and get my tummy rubbed. A day in the life of a cat is full of pleasure.

Lorna McCole (10)
Overtown Primary School

A Day In The Life Of The House Cat

Hello, let me introduce myself, I am Midnight Johnson, a black house cat and I would like to tell you about a day in my life to show you how my life works.

First of all I woke up with the sun in my deep green eyes, I squinted and turned my head away. Then I heard Mrs Johnson call Jack and Jill down for breakfast. Breakfast! Yum! I hopped off of Mrs Johnson's bed and scampered down the stairs to the kitchen. I miaowed quietly and Jill threw me down a piece of her toast. Jill and I always do that, it's our little secret! I felt myself being lifted up, then I realised Mrs Johnson was lifting me, she held me very tightly. Her gentle hands stroking my back very lightly and softly.

She put me down onto the floor and opened the back door to let me out for some fresh air. I saw something move in the long green grass, so I slowly moved closer, my tail twitched, my eyes grew wild with excitement, then, at the last minutes, I pounced! I saw before me a small black and white bird, I think it was a sparrow, but I lifted my paw to check and it flew away. Well there goes my dinner, I thought, as I watched the small bird fly into the distance. I'm stuck with cat food again!

I looked up at Jack and Jill's old brown shed, I started to climb the ladders that leant against the shed, when I heard a deep growl. Oh no! It's Dynamite, the dog next door, he's a big black Doberman with teeth as sharp as a knife! I scrambled up the ladder and hissed. I threw a paw down and scratched him right on his big black nose! He whimpered and ran into his house. Phew! I thought. I curled up and fell fast asleep and when I woke up it was pitch-black. I stretched my slender body and ran up to the back door and started miaowing loudly. I heard footsteps, then Mrs Johnson opened the door and lifted me up. She carried me upstairs to her bed and sat me on the bottom of it. As I curled up I said to myself 'Just a normal day in Midnight Johnson's life!'

Nicole Sommerville (10)
Overtown Primary School

A Day In The Life Of A Dog

Hi! My name is Robbie. I am a 16-week-old Yorkie pup. I have a brother and a master and I love them very much. My brother is older than I am so that makes me the runt of the litter. My master's name is Alexander and my brother's name is Prince.

I try to go out every morning and do my toilet but sometimes I'm a tiny bit naughty and do it on my master and on the floor! When I come back in, my food is always waiting. Mmm, yum, my favourite, chicken breast. When I am a good boy I get lots of treats and attention.

Yesterday Prince and I chased off a bunch of pigeons. We've had lots of adventures. Our most scary one was when I got chased by a huge, horrible bloodthirsty, scary black Labrador bitch. I squealed for my brother and master whilst her jaws were closing on me. My master finally came for me and he jumped over the fence, grabbed me and ran out of the gate.

Have I mentioned my friend Big Jay? He's a black Labrador and very protective. There's only one thing I hate and that's getting my horrible yucky worming stuff. When Alexander gets back from school I squeal with excitement and jump up on his leg, knowing it's playtime!

I love my family and I'm happy where I live!

Alexander Dickson (10)
Overtown Primary School

A Day In The Life Of A Cat

Hello! My name is Salem. I am a two year old street cat. I have magical powers, I can travel in time and I can talk to people.

I am the leader of a cat gang, I can help people if they want to be young again, even teachers!

I go out at night to look for people, but sometimes I look for them in the morning as well. One day I found a teacher who wanted to be young again, so I jumped on to her and we jumped into the past. When she was a child she was happy and had fun with her friends. She loved being a child.

Then she was so sad because she missed being a teacher and missed the children, so she wanted to go back home but she didn't know how to get back. Then I came and jumped on to her and we went back to the present. She was a teacher again.

Now I'm not a street cat anymore, because I am staying with the teacher.

Pamela Murdoch (10)
Overtown Primary School

A Day In The Life Of A Car

Hello, my name is Clio and I am a little silver car. I have an owner and I have a friend beside me, but he is faster and older than I am. He beats me all the time when we have a race, Oh, I nearly forgot, my owner's name is Charles.

I am driven on Mondays to Fridays and I am happy. But on the other two days I have a rest. When I have no petrol left, we go to the garage and get more. When I get petrol it's like a drink to me.

On holidays, I drive my owners to the airport and when they take off I feel lonely, but when they come back I am happy. When we get back home, I am back to normal.

I like it where I stay, and I get to play with my friend beside me. I love my owner and I am not lonely when I see him. I think I have a good life, but I don't like getting wet.

Ross Hadfield (10)
Overtown Primary School

A Day In The Life Of A Squirrel

Hello, my name is Carla and I am timid. I live in a tall tree in a deep wood. My friends live across the river in Acorn Woods and I haven't seen them for a month.

I eat nuts and bits of bramble, I really like nuts, I always collect them in my house all the time.

Now that I have finished my lunch, I think I should go to the river and drink some water. Slurp, slurp, slurp. Ahh! That was good.

When I was little, my mum always told me to climb trees and now I am fast at climbing. I really love my mum. Yesterday I saved a little bird from the magpies who were killing it. I was a brave squirrel.

It is dark and I think I should go to bed and take a nap for a while and I hope I will get some beauty sleep. I hope I will (yawn) see you again. Zzzzzzzzzz.

Victoria Sing (10)
Overtown Primary School

A DAY IN THE LIFE OF AN EXPLORER

Hello, my name is Simon Berret. I am an explorer of the . . . everything really! At the moment I am on my ship The Adventurer. I am working with my compass and map. We are trying to look for new land. Hold on a minute, my crew-member Bob is shouting at me 'We've spotted land Sir! Right over there. Look!' I'd better go and get my things ready, we're going to explore!

The land is beautiful. I have found a temple. I think I have got all my tools out now and I am scratching away all the mud, sand and horrible stuff! There are beautiful markings and old ancient writing I think it is. There are swirls and squiggles and oh, what's this? Something shiny. Hhhh! It's gold! It's sparkling and I can't believe it. 'We've found more over here Sir!' It's a miracle. I'm going to be rich. What a wonderful day, let's see if there's any more. How exciting, it is the best day of my life!

I have just seen a tiger, it was growling but it never attacked anyone. It's strange, there was a monkey on its back. It was as if they were friends.

After a hard day's exploring, I tuck myself into my sleeping bag and look at the stars. I just wonder what tomorrow will have in store for me!

Leigh McDonald (10)
Overtown Primary School

A Day In The Life Of A Bird

Hello, my name is Sally Sparrow.

My day starts off with me having to go and look for worms for my young. I live in a big place called Motherwell, I live in a little nest in a big tree. Today some of my eggs are supposed to hatch and I am very excited!

I think I will go down to the garden to get some worms. Oh no! Here comes the cat, it's going to get me! I will need to fly as fast as I can, and look! There's a magpie going into my nest. I hope he will not hurt any of my babies.

Oh look! My oldest one has just started to fly, that means that we can go south for the winter. Oh where is one of my babies? Oh look! My baby is down on the grass. *Watch out for that cat!* I thought I told you not to go out of the nest!

Now it's time for my young to go to bed and sleep. I will sing them a song to get them to sleep and when I go to bed I will think of what tomorrow may bring. I hope that it will be a great day.

Gemma Burns (10)
Overtown Primary School

A Day In The Life Of Santa

On a cold winter morning Santa woke up early between the hours of six and seven. He woke up this early because he had to make and wrap all the toys. Mary woke about 8.30am. She had to bake all the cakes and put up all the decorations.

When they were both up and dressed they got to work. Santa called his elves to come and help. Meanwhile Mary was busy preparing the cakes.

Over the last week, Santa had received lots of lists from excited children. Santa had lots of toys to make, like dolls, horses, bats, balls, teddies and trains.

About 1.45pm Mary called 'Lunchtime!' and Santa and his twenty-five elves came running into the kitchen. They had a very big lunch to build up their energy. After lunch, they got back to work. After about another three hours, they had finished. But still no stopping. Santa had to polish Rudolf's nose to make it shine.

Mary called to Santa, 'Come! Come and see what I have done!' Mary had put up the decorations. The room was a beautiful sight to see. Santa sat down and yawned. At the end of a tiring day, Santa and Mary went for a good rest.

Rachel Smith (9)
Ralston Primary School

A Day In The Life Of A Pig

In my day I eat barley and I am put in a sty every day. It is just like a giant mud pit. It is very dirty and there are about one hundred pigs in one sty! We all fight for food, we would eat all day if we were allowed to. Nothing exciting really happens to me as I am always locked up.

One day I watched some men coming to visit the farm where I lived. After a few hours the men came back and I knew it had something to do with the pain I was in. I had blisters in my mouth and on my feet and when I looked around the other pigs looked the same.

As the men examined us again I knew there was something bad going on. I had never felt as bad as this before in my life. I feared the worst for me and the other pigs. Then I heard one of the men say we had foot and mouth. Later on that day we were all gathered together. The pigs in front of me were taken away one by one. I saw men in big suits in case they caught the disease, they had masks over their faces. As I got nearer to the front of the line, I could hear shots and I could hear the other pigs squealing. When I came to the front of the line there was a man standing with a needle. Then stop. I was put down.

Jamie Hamilton (9)
Ralston Primary School

A Day In The Life Of My Sister

Hi! I am Rachael, I have just got out of my bed. I am going downstairs now for my breakfast. I am having Coco Pops, these are lovely! I have finished now and I had better get ready. What will I wear? I know! I'll wear my pink top and black trousers. At last I'm ready.

I'm going to get my sister up at my cousin's house today. My mum is taking me and we're going now. We're going up the hill and now we're here. I'm going in now . . . 'Hello! Victoria is already here, I'm picking her up. Come on Victoria, Mum is taking us home now.'
'Okay!'

We have left the house and we are on our way home. I'm going back in the house and Victoria and I are fighting over whose turn it is on the computer. I wish Victoria would just give me a turn.

Just then my dad came in and told us he needed the computer to do some work on. Why does Dad have so much work?

I think I'll draw a picture because I'm bored. Victoria is watching the TV but it is something I hate that is on, so I'm going to bed.

I'm putting my pyjamas on now and . . . I'm ready. I'm going to watch Sleeping Beauty. I'm getting tired now so . . . goodnight!

Victoria Ross (11)
Ralston Primary School

A Day In The Life Of Bart Simpson

Yawn! I have just got out of bed and I am now going downstairs to bug Lisa and get some breakfast. There is nothing to eat because Homer has already eaten a whole box of cereal and Lisa has just left for school. Talking about school, I'd better go.

Mum has made me a big lunch so I grabbed it and ran to try and catch the bus. On the way to school Otto the driver had been speeding so we were chased by the cops. Otto lost them, but we were late for school.

When we got to school there was a book report (I'd completely forgotten). Principle Skinner put the reports in alphabetical order. I love being a Simpson.

Right - no As so straight to the Bs. Bart! Oh no! Ringgg. Saved by the bell, there was a fire. Well not really! It was only Jimbo and Nelson, the school bullies messing about. Principle Skinner then called a meeting in the Assembly about fires, but I wasn't really listening. He eventually stopped talking. He was talking all afternoon, so it was time to go home.

When I got home I phoned Moe's bar.
'Hello, how can I help you?' he said.
'Can I talk to an Oproblem, Bee Oproblem?'
Then he said to the people in the bar 'There's someone looking for an Oproblem, Bee Oproblem, come on guys, do I have a Bee Oproblem in here?'
Then someone said 'You sure do!'
I put the phone down and ran to my bedroom. I looked at my clock it was 11.00pm and I went to bed and nodded off.

Niall Kelly (11)
Ralston Primary School

A Day In The Life Of A Teacher

Oh, I'm so tired - didn't get much sleep last night. Anyway I can't lie in bed all day. Okay, I think I'll put on my yellow top today, it might brighten me up a bit.

I put on my yellow top, navy skirt and navy shoes. I feel a little less sleepy now. Don't feel much like breakfast this morning, just have a glass of fresh orange.

Now I'm in the car, still nearly falling asleep. It's 8.45 and I'm still on the motorway!

Okay now I'm in school, just putting my bag down when Alison McGhee put a letter about York on my desk, it's still only 8.57, school hasn't even started yet! Sometimes I think these children are on a different planet!

I've done the register and lunches, now we're off to maths, so that went okay. Now at last a bit of time to myself - a cup of tea, and a big fat pile of jotters to mark. This just isn't my day, is it?

I'm back in the classroom working on topic work with the children, they have their hands up constantly asking pointless questions! Sometimes I do wonder! They are out for lunch now, thank heavens!

They're back. Oh lucky me! Everyone immediately starts talking - cheek! I settle them down to some maths until home time, that's not a problem, just a few moans and groans.

Now I'm going to have a bath, a chocolate bar, the OK magazine and an early night. What a day!

Janey Chalmers (12)
Ralston Primary School

A Day In The Life Of A Dog

Woof! Woof! Grr! The dog growls at someone coming in with another dog.
'Wow, boy!' says the owner 'I would like you to meet Sparkie, Honey and Groucher.'
'Grr!'
'I don't think he likes them do you?'
'He'll get along with them some day.'
'Prrr, we'd better be quiet, he gets angry when anyone wakes him up.'
Woof! Woof! Grrr!
Another dog walks by and barks.

The owner gets lunch ready for the dogs when they wake up.
'Do you want anything to eat or drink?'
'No thanks,' she said 'I am taking the dogs out for a walk. Do you want to come? We'll take my dogs if you want.'
'I have to go home at a quarter past six so we'll have to be sharp on getting home.'
'You can phone your mum on my mobile if you want to stay out later.'
'Though my dinner is already put out anyway, I'd better get heading home now.'
'So you can't stay out later?'
'No, sorry about that. I will be out tomorrow walking my dog if you want to come out.'
'No, I can't I am going to my gran's.'
Chap! Chap! Chap!
'Hello!'
'Go away!'

Neil Bennett
Ralston Primary School

A Day In The Life Of An Ant

Work, work, work. I'm like a slave. Building tunnels, carrying stuff seven times my own body weight. You may think it's cool, it's anything but that!

The queen! Don't get me started on her, she's all 'Do this, do that'! Mind you it must be hard, she has a baby every second or so! Anyway I must get off, I've got work to do. My group is the first when searching for food. The danger is . . . you! You humans! What did we ever do to you? Especially the small ones. Stomp, stomp, all day long. It's tough being an ant, so think about us before you stomp.

Anyway, here goes, nothing. Aha! There's an apple. Let's get it! Across the grass, mud and gravel we went. Yes! We got it. Oooh no! It's humans. It's a trap. Here comes the feet. Duck! Another duck! Get out of here. Oh no, they're chasing us. Ahh, run!

I got away, but some of my group wasn't so lucky. I went home and alarmed the queen's guards. Now I've to do tree duty. I've just got to look at the holes in the trees to make sure there is no blockage. Easy peasy. No danger here . . . Ahh, it's the kids with the water guns. I'll get into this hole here. They've spotted me . . . Swoosh!

Andrew Carruthers (11)
Ralston Primary School

A Day In The Life Of A Computer

Here they come, coming up the stairs to turn me on and go on the Internet probably.

Yes, I was right. Here they are, ready to press the button to turn me on. Wah! I'm being moved. I was wrong!

I am in a van now and being sent to a house. I think I heard a man say. Wait a minute, we have stopped. We must be at that house thing I heard that guy talking about. What a fancy house, I do hope this is it.

My dreams have come true, I am wired up and ready to run in my new home. I have a boy playing me now, he hits my keyboard too hard, but who cares? I am having the best time of my life in this wonderland called a house.

The boy has now left me and gone to bed, and the mum is now playing me, she has connected to the Internet and gone to WWW.Hotmail.com she has some very rude e-mails. I wish you could see them!

I think that this could be my destiny to stay in this house and to be used every minute of the day.

I love the whole family except the barking dog!

Blair Stevenson (12)
Ralston Primary School

A DAY IN THE LIFE OF A BABY

Hello everyone, it's me, Beth. I'm about to tell you what happened yesterday, you won't believe it . . .

Well that night I had a dream that I wished to be a baby for one day, and yes, you've guessed it, it came true. I woke up next morning in a cot beside my best friend's bed, she was all grown up and had a husband and everything. Her name's Janey and her husband (my dad) was called Richard. She lifted me out of the cot and dressed me in a pink dress and a matching hat, it was so cute. She then put me in a pram and took me to my nursery, where there were lots of children. I thought it would be great, but I was wrong because the children were nasty, they stole my lunch and toys.

As soon as nursery finished I got loads of sweets. It was great, although I was sick and I had to go to the doctors and get a jab. I have a phobia about jabs, so I started to cry and I fainted, but then I was fine. Mum kept hugging me and talking baby talk. I could not understand her. She took me home for my tea and it was mushy peas and mashed potatoes, ughh! I went to sleep and woke up in my usual bed. I'm sure it wasn't a dream. Or maybe it was!

Beth Mullaney (11)
Ralston Primary School

A Day In The Life Of Myself

One summer's day at 7 o'clock, my dad said 'Get up, lazy bones.'
I said 'Why? It is summer today?'

I get dressed and then I have my breakfast and a drink of sweet organic orange juice. I play the PlayStation until somebody comes in for me and I go out to play. Then, me and all my friends play football, and sometimes a game of Records. If you volley the ball in the goals, you get a point, or if you head the ball, you get another point. If the keeper catches it, then you go in goal and if it goes by, you still go in.

Craig is good at crossing the ball. I am quite good as well. I don't usually score but I set a lot up. I hardly ever go in the goal because I usually don't miss my chances. It is a very good game that I enjoy a lot. It is quite hard to score into the keeper, if they are brilliant at catching the ball, like Craig is.

Suddenly the rain came down very heavily and we went into my friend's house and it rained for ten minutes. Then we went back outside again and played a game of Records and Craig fell over the ball, but I still scored into Jordan, who is another one of my friends.

I really enjoy playing with my friends because they like football as well.

Gavin Hair (12)
Ralston Primary School

A Day In The Life Of A Coin!

I'm a coin, a pound coin to be precise, I've just been made so I'm all gold and shiny. The only thing I don't like about being a pound is that I've got the Queen's head on my belly and when someone touches me it tickles.

'Hey, it's dark in here.' Oh yes, we're in the big van being taken to different shops. I wonder what shop I'll be going to. I'm kind of squashed just now because we are all in long lines together.

Oh well, I got in the till in Woolworth's. It's even darker in here than it was in the van. 'He, he, he,' that tickles. I can see the light. I must be going away again. Yes, I am right. I'm in a red leather purse and it really smells in here. Has she never heard of air freshener or perfume? It's quite fun bouncing along in a purse and you don't even know where you're going or where you are.

Aaaahhh! I've just been dropped. Has she noticed? Yes. I see her walking away. I'm now in a ripped hat. Oh, now I get it, I'm in a homeless person's hat. Is he going to eat me? No, thank goodness. He's just looking at my gleam. Oh no, I'm rolling and rolling and I can't stop. Plop! Yes, you guessed it, I rolled into a drain. I'll never get found down here. What a day for a new pound coin!

Hannah van Hombergh (11)
Ralston Primary School

A Day In The Life Of A Pound Coin

Hello, I'm a pound coin. I just woke up in the purse (my home). The purse is going to something called shops. I'm going now. I'm in the car and I'm bouncing along, the purse and I don't like it.

'It's stuffy in here. I want out.' We are, oh I mean I'm at shops.

'Air, thank you Mrs Green.' Oh so this is shops. A person is standing behind a big desk with a whatever it is, I don't know, thing. Mrs Green picks up her milk and hands it over to the person behind the desk and me also. She puts me in the till, well at least that's what she calls it. I meet lots of 2ps, 5ps, £1, £2, 10ps etc. They hate me though.

Here comes Mrs Brown (Mrs Green's neighbour).

She gets her bread and gives it to the person. Unfortunately I am not her change. A 10p and 2p are her change. 'Please get me out of here. It's nothing like the purse.'

Mrs White is here now and I know what she's going to get. A card for her son's wedding, whatever that is. Mrs Green's forgotten something and she's back to get it. Teabags I suppose. She always forgets them. Oh no! Here comes Madame Valenti, but what's she doing here? I thought she hated it here and went to 'so you think you're rich' shopping centre. I am her change and I went into her big handbag and into her new purse. She is now off to Mrs Visage, or in other words, Mrs Face to have her face done again. I am being given to Mrs Visage. She's okay, I suppose. I get put in her pocket.
'Bonjour, come with me,' said Mrs Visage's assistant. I just happen to know that Madame Valenti is a witch.

She went into a dark room and lay back while Mrs Visage peeled her face off and washed it. Strangely enough Mrs Green appeared and paid her cash. I was her change. Hooray! I'm back in the purse. Phew, what a journey I've had.

Rachel Monteith (11)
Ralston Primary School

A Day In The Life Of An American Cent . . .

Ching, ching, light, yes, maybe I'll be taken out this time! Bang. The till was shut again. Am I going to be stuck in here forever?

Zzzzzz. Ching, ching. Woooo and I was plunged into total darkness. I had been taken out of the till and was in a man's pocket. Gun shots rang out along with terrified screams!
'Empty your pockets and give me your money!'
The store was being robbed. I was tumbling into a bag and heard a car revving. It was comforting to know I was good enough to be stolen. It was exciting to be in on the life of crime.

A lot later we were driving by the house of George W Bush, the president of the United States of America, when one of the robbers flipped me out of the window shouting, 'Here's a little present before we kill you! Ha, ha!' and they sped off.

I lay there until the president came along. He was on a little stroll before dinner, anyway he picked me up for luck and put me in his chest pocket. Bang! A gun shot was fired. Clunk! There was the sound of metal hitting metal at a fast speed. It was me! We were falling backwards. I thought I was going to die but then I remembered I was metal. Now I have a very pretty dent in me but I'm happy 'cause I saved the president's life. I am his lucky cent!

Ashleigh Welsh (12)
Ralston Primary School

A Day In The Life Of My Dog Trixie

I get my breakfast, then I go out for walkies with my owner. When I come home I go out to play with my owner. When I get tired I go for my morning nap 'til twelve o'clock when I get my dinner. After I get my dinner I go outside and sit down for a while.

When my owner finishes her dinner we go outside and play football. When she gets bored of it we go in and play the PlayStation fighting game. I've got 200 points just now! Then we go for the afternoon walkies to Penilee Park. I go back home and sit in the wheelbarrow and my owner pushes me around the patio. Then I go to the shops with my owner and she buys me doggie biscuits, yum. I go for my nap and my owner wakes me up in time for my programme that I like. Tom And Jerry. I like watching the cat get beaten up by the mouse.

I get my tea then have a game of fetch. I go to bed at nine o'clock while my owner watches TV. I sit on the top of her cover 'til she comes in to give me a kiss on the nose. I give her a lick then settle down beside her.

Danielle Craig (11)
Ralston Primary School

A DAY IN THE LIFE OF JENNIFER ANISTON

I woke up this morning with somebody banging on my door shouting, 'Get up, get up.' It was 5.30am, so I went and opened the door. It was my make-up artist to do my make-up because we were starting to film a new series of Friends.

I had just had all my make-up put on. I felt like I had a face on my face. Yuk! 6.01am. Then I had to get dressed. I was put in black trousers and a black shirt, plus black dolly shoes, it was okay, not my sort of thing.

6.20am. Time to start filming. I met the rest of the crew there as usual. I was late. We filmed for most of the day. We stopped for lunch. Matt who plays Joey came to lunch with me. We went to a lovely little cafe.

We both had a chicken sandwich, it was brilliant. Then after that we had to go back for more filming, boring!

When we got back I had to get more make-up on, and on top of that a chicken suit, because we were at the part where Ross needed a big fluffy chicken to come and scare away birds that were nesting at his house, so I had to do it. It was horrible! We went on filming late into the night.

When I got home I went straight to my bed.

Kaye McKinlay (12)
Ralston Primary School

A Day In The Life Of A Shoe!

One hot and sunny morning, the doors of the cupboard swung open. I was hoping it would be my turn. I saw the hand reaching for me. I was so happy. I couldn't wait. It was my turn finally! On I went, but suddenly, the foot, so smelly, I forgot she sometimes put me on after she had been running. I was unhappy because I would have to sit for hours with this horrible stink. It smelt like old mouldy cheese.

Then we started to move. Up the stairs we went, then into the bathroom. Maybe this time she will wash her feet and they will be clean. But, no. She was only washing her hands. So back into the room we went. She took me off and then I saw a clean pair of socks. She took the old smelly ones off and put on the nice new clean ones. Then she slipped me back on. It still smelled a little bit but it was better than before. So we went back down the stairs. We sat for hours and hours and the smell got worse and worse. I was tired and I was feeling sick. Suddenly, up we got, up the stairs, was she washing her feet? Then we went into the bedroom, oh no, she was taking me off. I was so sad but it was getting late so back into the cupboard I went. That was a day in the life of a shoe!

Fiona McKenzie (11)
Ralston Primary School

A Day In The Life Of My Rat

Hello, my name is Homer. I am 19 weeks old and I am about 23cm long. People are afraid of me because of my tail. My owner walks through the door without feeding me and out again, although I was fed in the morning, but not very much. My brother Bart is very timid and gentle and won't hurt a fly.

I am hungry! Hurry up and feed me! Change my water and give me my vitamins! Yes, I'm out of my cage. Oh no! I'm getting photos taken! Oh, wait a minute, that means chocolate buttons to get me to stay still! I'm getting my training now. I climb stairs, go through tubes and hang upside down with my tail on someone's finger and I jump hurdles. After all that I get one chocolate button. Then my mum takes me into the living room and sits down and I fall asleep on her lap. I fall asleep for half an hour, then get taken back to my cage. Then I get my food and I get my vitamins and water changed. At night I get washed with a wet towel and my cage cleaned out. Someone comes in the room, turns on the light, says goodnight and then the light goes off again and I fall asleep.

Stephanie Breslin (10)
Ralston Primary School

A Day In The Life Of Mini The Mouse

Hello everybody. My name is Mini the mouse and I know what you're all thinking, but no, I'm not Mickey's wife. I don't even know Mickey or Minnie! Anyway, I'm called Mini the mouse because I am the smallest and the youngest in my family. We live at 229 Glasgow Road in a mouse hole in the Montgomery's house. I have two big brothers, two big sisters, a mum and a dad.

Anyway, I am going to tell you what happened today, just go to the next chapter.

I woke up early this morning because I heard a peculiar noise outside our mouse hole. I went out to see what it was. It was my dad cutting the carpet. I had my breakfast, my favourite mouldy Swiss cheese. Well I like anything that's mouldy. I know what you're thinking, I know I'm weird. After my breakfast I went and told my mum that I was going out to play with Tortella the tortoise. She was the Montgomery's pet tortoise.

I quickly brushed my teeth, washed my face, went out and up the stairs to meet Tortella.

She had come out of her house to meet me and we went out into the back garden and played for a while. Then we went back to our house to get dinner and guess what? I had mouldy Swiss cheese, two helpings.

After dinner Mum told me I had to go to bed and I drifted off to cheese land.

Deborah Montgomery (11)
Ralston Primary School

A DAY IN THE LIFE OF A GOSHAWK

I was awakened by a little sound and at the speed of light I opened my eyes and swooped down looking for the creature that had woken me up. Then I saw it. A rabbit! I dived for it and dug my claws into it and it struggled to get free. I thought it was wasting its energy and I was right. It tried to jump but when it jumped I dug my claws deeper into it and slashed its heart and it died. I pecked at it, getting nice, fresh meat. I started to rip it in half to get even more juicy meat. Ten minutes later there was one piece of meat left and just as I was about to eat it a sparrow hawk swooped down and took it. I raced for the meat and successfully snatched it from the hawk, but I was still hungry. I looked for that sparrow hawk who had snatched the meat from me and luckily I saw him eating a field mouse. I swooped down and started a fight. I got cut but he lost an eye, although both of us were injured he came off worse. I had used the same strategy that I had used with the rabbit. I tried to fly back to my family, but I was too weak so I called for my wife. 'Aawwwkkk!' My wife came to me and helped me home. I was so weak from the battle I couldn't sleep that night. Then a noise woke me.

Coooo. It was an owl. It was attacking my wife but I couldn't help her because I was so tired. I saw a mouse scurrying in the field below so I gathered all my energy to swoop down. I went beak first and killed it but the owl saw me and he came after me. I kept on dodging the owl then I flew to a tall tree. The owl came after me. I moved out of the way and the owl hit the tree and was knocked out. All the other birds in the forest were looking at me and thought I was the best fighter ever to live. They thought I would go down in bird history. After a long day I was exhausted like a bird without wings. I flew back to my nest and curled up into a ball and went to sleep wondering what was coming tomorrow.

Stewart Roy (9)
Rosewell Primary School

TONY HAWKS - A WORTHY ROLE MODEL

Tony Hawks is a famous skateboarder who is the world's number one within professional skateboarding. He has blue eyes, black hair and a skull skateboard with red wheels which can reach top speeds when he is attempting various specialised tricks. He has a really kind heart for people all over the world. He also gives to the poor and raises funds for different charities. He lives in Beverly Hills and he has a swimming pool and a tennis court in his garden. Tony Hawks also has a Ferrari and a Porsche which he uses to travel around in with his wife and children. Tony Hawks travels throughout Europe with his best friend Andrew Reynolds, and they visit all the different skate parks throughout the world, competing in competitions with other professional skateboarders.

Tony Hawks owns twenty-five different skateboards with different patterns on each of them. He also enjoys poetry and reads from a wide selection of books, which are kept within his library in his house. He also enjoys creative writing and drawing.

Tony has a large wardrobe of designer suits, some of which have skateboard designs on them, and he also collects different types of shoes and skateboards. He has collected twenty-six trophies, and he has become very wealthy due to the prize money that he has collected from winning various competitions.

Andrew Hewitson (11)
St Mark's Primary School, Irvine

THE DREAM

There was a girl from Scotland called Delphinium, that was Greek for a little dolphin. She had always wanted to swim with dolphins. One year she went to Florida on holiday with her family. She found a gold coin - it was a magic coin.

She said, 'I wish I could be a dolphin for a day.' She got her wish - it was fascinating. Her hair vanished, she had soft skin that was blue with a touch of grey. Delphinium's voice became squeaky. The sea was a noisy place - she could hear clicks, squeaks, whistles, grunts, and even chuckles.

She said, 'I like being a dolphin. I can leap and somersault when I play and swim very, very fast.' She was hungry and had to dive down deep into the sea to catch food. Delphinium used her teeth to catch the slippery fish but she couldn't chew them. She had to swallow the fish whole and raw, yuk!

She saw coral reefs like rainbows and all kinds of fish that looked yummy!

Suddenly it was time to swim back to the shore - she made it just in time.

Heather Martin (11)
St Mark's Primary School, Irvine

A DAY IN THE LIFE OF MY COMPUTER

Today I got loaded up by Dad and my cables were hard at work, he was doing a schedule. I had to load up Word for him to do it. He had to change the font, no I'm wrong, *I* had to change the font. Dad's finished the schedule and he's coming off. He gets out of the chair, walks out of the room, he's going, going, gone, you are the weakest link, goodbye!

Now it's time to surf the net all by myself! Hey, I'm a magic computer! I have a golf game loaded up on me so I'm going to *WWW.Golfskills.com* to brush up on my game, hopefully I'll get birdies on every hole. Whoops, sorry, dreaming a bit there! Right, time to get off, Isabella might be wondering where I am, that's my girlfriend, she's my screensaver. I always send her a message on Fridays. Oh well, I'm going to sleep. It's been a hard morning, night-night.

I'm up and feeling a bit sick, but never fear, the doc's here! Okay, I'm feeling bright and breezy. I'm having a wee cup of tea with the internet and then I'll have another little nap but I'll enjoy this first.

Ahhh, powercut, zzzzzz!

Alan Murdoch (11)
Sheuchan Primary School

A Day In The Life Of A Dolphin

I live in Dolphin Cove with my pals. Here every dolphin has a pen of its own. This is our routine for the day:

George the park keeper comes to wake us up round about sunrise. We get fed a big bucket of fish, individually, which is usually cod. George gets really tired after he's fed us our breakfast. Then he lets us swim around with the other dolphins.

George gives us a practise by calling out the names of the tricks.

When he opens the park, quite a lot of people enter. George puts on some music and he starts shouting the names of the tricks like spyhops, belly flops and the hoop jump. We obey and start our tricks. It's really fun, but when we did the belly flop, my best friend hurt herself so she couldn't do any more tricks for the next week.

The park closes for lunch. Thank goodness, I'm starving. George comes round with a big bucket of fish, this time it's haddock for a change.

George opens the park again. He puts on the music and starts shouting the names of the tricks again. When I had to do the hoop jump, I hurt my spine really badly.

George wouldn't let me go out for two months. It's really sore and it's sore when I move too. I get medicine for it, but it's a syringe they give me. I hate them. It helps me to get better so I put up with it.

After the two months I was much better and now I can go and do tricks again.

George was really kind and understanding. He's the best keeper any dolphin could have.

Kirsty McKerrow (11)
Sheuchan Primary School

A Day In The Life Of Hannah

At 7.00 I wake up and get dressed. I put on my denim, baggy pedal pushers and my pink twin set (strap top and cardigan) since it is a sunny day outside.

I go downstairs and have breakfast, it's toast. Then I ask Mum to do my hair in a ponytail. Next thing on my schedule is, mmmm, let me think, Dad's washing the car with Christopher and Mum's ironing, so it means it's time for me to phone Kimberley to ask if she wants to go down town.

'Mum, I'm going to phone Kimberley.'
'Okay.'
I dial the number, 7-0-3-0-1-0, bring, bring, bring, bring.
'Hello?'
'Hello Jenni, can I speak to Kimberley,'
'Yeah, I'll just get her for you.'
'Thanks.'
I wait for a few minutes and then hear a familiar voice.
'Hello? Hello Kimberly?'
'Oh, hello'
'Do you want to go down town this afternoon?'
'Yeah, okay, what time?'
'About 3.00, while the dads are at the football?'
'Fine with me.'
'Okay, see you then.'
Time speeds by and before long I am sitting in Petrucci's having a coke. I check my watch. It's 4.30, Kimberley and I catch the west end bus back to her house. Our mums are sitting waiting for us. They tell us we're all having tea at Kimberley's house, it's a Chinese carryout. We eat tea and beg our mums to let us stay at each other's house, they finally give in and I stay at Kimberley's house overnight.

Kimberley Murray (11)
Sheuchan Primary School

A DAY IN THE LIFE OF A LEOPARD

'Mum, I hear a noise, what is it?' asked Kala.
'I don't know, but it doesn't matter,' replied her mum.
'Oh please can I go and find out, please, please, please,' begged Kala.
'No, it's time for your bath in the river,' said her mum.
Kala was really determined to find out what the noise was, so she went out when her mum was having an afternoon nap.

Kala rustled through the bushes until she came to where the sound was coming from. She kept going until she saw a baby elephant, so she decided to chase it instead. Once the chase was over, Kala realised she was lost.

'Mum,' Kala shouted in her loudest voice but there was no reply. Kala went deeper and deeper into the jungle until she came to a safari park. She had to keep herself hidden or the other animals would eat her.

Kala heard voices coming her way, she ran as fast as her little legs could carry her, then she heard footsteps coming towards her. She stopped. A little girl picked her up. She cried and roared for help. She called on her mum but she didn't get an answer.
'It's okay,' said the little girl. 'I'll look after you.'

The little girl took Kala home and shut the door because she didn't want her mum to know about this.

When the little girl was at school Kala tried to escape but failed. She was really missing her family but no one knew if she would get home.

Jasmin Chung (11)
Sheuchan Primary School

A DAY IN THE LIFE OF DAISY THE BUTTERFLY

It was a beautiful summer's morning and all Daisy could hear was the very light wind rustling against the leaves of the prickly rose bush where Daisy rested.

She later decided to take advantage of no one being up, especially that two year old, Lucy. She always thinks Daisy is a toy. After about ten minutes she heard squeals and giggles coming out of the house.

At that point she quickly scrambled around in the rose bush gathering up as much food as she could. When the 'humans' had finished their breakfast, Lucy and Marie were mucking about with their see-saw.

Disaster, Lucy had clapped her eyes on Daisy. Thank goodness it takes her about ten minutes to stand up, so Daisy had got well into next door's garden.

While she was next door she decided to have a rest and make the most of the peace and quiet. When she fluttered her way back to her bush she discovered that the 'human's' cat, Molly, was sitting on the wall behind her bush and that Molly had a habit of eating flying things.

Daisy felt two green eyes staring at her, even though she was looking at one of her own caterpillars. The insect-eating animal pounced, but Daisy managed to flutter away.

Caitlin Dampney (12)
Sheuchan Primary School

A Day In The Life Of A Fish

Lauren woke up to the sound of her mobile. It was a text message from her best friend Hazel asking her if she wanted to go down the street. Lauren texted Hazel back to say she would meet her at 11.00.

Lauren got out of bed, got changed and had breakfast. Then she put her money and mobile into her bag and waited for Hazel to come for her.

Lauren sat down and watched the television. The next thing she knew she had gills, fins and scales. She was a fish, and a shark was heading straight for her. She quickly darted behind some coral. Lauren looked out into the sea from between the fingers of coral. The shark had gone. Just at that moment she was in Britain not America.

Lauren wondered what she was going to do, how was she going to get to be a human again and how could she get food while avoiding sharks and fishing nets? She thought to herself, what do fish eat? I know, seaweed. Now to find some seaweed, oh there's some.

What's happening! Where am I going? I'm in a net, oh no, I'm in a net. Help! Help! Here's a hole, I'll just slip through it. I'm small enough, am I?

Phew, that was close!

It was just then that Hazel knocked on the door and Lauren realised it was only a daydream.

Clare Wilson (11)
Sheuchan Primary School

A Day In The Life Of Tober The Horse

I woke up early one morning, ate some grass and stretched my legs. I then went for a short gallop around the field, came back and woke up Tara (my best friend) and we went for a race around the field. Tara won because she is an Anglo-Arab and I am a Welsh Mountain horse. We went back to eat some grass and we could hear the dogs barking. It was a lovely day so we went to lie in the sun and the grass was wet.

'In about ten minutes we will be going for a ride with Leanne,' Tara reminded me.

'I know,' I replied.

It was about lunch time, we had just finished our walk. Leanne took off our equipment and groomed us. We then went back to lie in the sun again. An hour later Leanne came over to give us some hard food. We finished and we were bored. We wished we were still in the big field because we have friends in the field next to it. Their names are Stally and Smokey.

After tea we went down past the loch, the deer park and back to the field. I was quite tired and Leanne brought us some more food. Then even more two hours later! This time it was vegetables which I don't like but they are healthy.

I had a nap for a couple of hours. We went back out, came back and went to sleep. Zzzzz.

Leanne McCrae (12)
Sheuchan Primary School

A Day In The Life Of T-Kay

In the mornings, I go to Toni's house to see her. She gives me food and lets me chase a lace and it's very good fun, she lets me sleep on her bed and look in all the rooms.

I hate it when she goes to school because I have nobody to play with. Round about 12.30pm I get bored of jumping for the little flies and eating them.

After a while, I go and play cat chase with the next door's dog. I think of it as a game but he just thinks of lunch. Yippee! Toni's home at last now, I won't be bored anymore. I wish she would hurry and open the door, oh no, she's going into the living room and now I won't be able to get in, but wait, here she comes, she's going into the cupboard. I'll jump onto the window sill and she'll see me and let me in.

I jumped up on to it and she opened the door so I ran in and up the stairs to find something to do. I went down the stairs to see Toni and she picked me up and gave me a cuddle. I jumped down and played cat chase with the dog. I ate some flies, ran around and went away to find something else to do. That's the day in the life of me - T-Kay.

Toni Savage (11)
Stanley Primary School

A Day In The Life Of A Penny

I am a penny and I live in the pocket of Jeremy Sprocket, I started in the Royal Mint. I then got passed on to a shop in a town near the factory.

A girl came into the shop and bought a stick of rock. She gave the owner a £5.00 note, but the rock cost 79p so she got four £1.00 coins, a 20p and me, a penny.

It did have to be me, the girl took me home and put me in her piggy bank. I met lots of my brothers and sisters. Not long after she brought me out of her bank and put me in her pocket with some other money. She took me to a shop and spent me, so I spent some time in a till.

A lady came into the shop to buy various groceries. Oh no! I was in with her change. She went home and gave her son his pocket money. The boy owed the dinner hall £1.19 so he gave them a £1.00 coin, a 10p piece, a 5p piece, a 2p piece, a lp piece and me.

Aaaahh! Jeremy Sprocket then got me from the dining hall, I wonder what will happen tomorrow?

Zoë Morrison (11)
Stanley Primary School

A Day In The Life Of Denver

Denver is my pet dog. He has never bitten anybody and he is very obedient. He likes women better than children but he loves playing with children. He doesn't like grown-up men, apart from Dad.

Denver has just woken up, he will wait patiently until someone takes him out. We usually take him down the burn. When we're walking him, he wants to go wherever you go.

When we leave for school, my sister and Dad look after him. They usually take him up to Raymond's house (my big brother). He has a dog (Tobi). Denver and Tobi will romp up and down the garden while Dad and Sharon have tea.

Then they might take him down to the beach. Sometimes Raymond and Tobi will go too. Denver plays fetch with a stick. He barks at the person who is holding the stick. He even swims in the water to get the stick. When he gets home he is exhausted but when we come in, he jumps around you so he gets a clap.

When we get our dinner, he always gets a bit, he eats meat but sometimes he eats chips. He'll get to go out again, then when he's sleeping, the house is calm and peaceful. As you can see a day in the life of Denver is never boring.

Paul Fitzpatrick (11)
Stanley Primary School

A Day In The Life OF A Pop Star

It's 6 o'clock on a Friday morning and Liza is rehearsing for tomorrow night's big event. It is the Royal Variety Performance and she is singing two of her number one songs, she is very excited and nervous. She has to perform in front of the Queen, Prince Charles and lots of other people. She is at vocal practise for two hours and then she will go to her choreographer to practice her dance routines.

She is now at the gym, Liza likes to keep fit and eat healthily. Liza is ready to go out for dinner with her famous boyfriend Ali G. It is the next morning and she is very anxious about tonight. She has to go to the doctor to see if her throat is OK to sing.

She has been to the gym, choreographer, doctor and vocal practise. She has even been to the concert hall as well to see her dressing room, costume and get used to everything on stage.

It is one hour away from the show, she looks at the timetable, first is Elton John, Westlife, Paul McCann, the hypnotist and then she is next. She came on stage and sang her songs, the audience and the Queen loved her.

She went to her dressing room and got changed and thought to herself, this has been a very exciting day and I will never forget it.

Natalie Campbell (12)
Stanley Primary School

A DAY IN THE LIFE OF A FOOTBALLER

It's the big day at Ibrox for me and the squad. At 8.30am I arrived to get ready for the cup. First I went to the physiotherapist to check my muscles. Then I went out to warm up. After 15 minutes Dick Advocaat, the coach, organised two teams. Then we went inside.

At 12 noon, the fans started to come. There were thousands of supporters and Dick said, 'Don't let them down!'

At 12.30pm we went out on to the pitch and signed some autographs. Then we did some stretches and went back in. At 1.00pm we went and got ready for kick off.

It was time for kick off at Ibrox, Tore Andre Flo and Rod Wallace are taking kick off at 1.15pm. The referee blew his whistle and we started the game. I pass to Wallace and he passes back to Stefan Klos so he could kick it up the field and it deflected and it was a corner. Albertz tooks it and I jumped up and scored. At half-time it was 3-0 to Rangers, Dick was delighted.

In the second half no one scored so it stayed at 3-0, we won the cup. Half an hour later, we went out to celebrate and get the cup. It was a fabulous day at Ibrox.

Cheryl Low (11)
Stanley Primary School

A Day In The Life Of A Footballer

I got up very early in the morning, so I could go to training. The training ground is far away from where I live. I'm the team captain. The coach phoned in sick so I had to take training, we had to train very hard because we had a big game the next day. We had to win the Scottish Cup against Celtic. My name is Giovanni Van Bronckhorst, I play for Rangers.

Today is the big match, it is live on television, I arrive at 8.00am and I'm the first one there. I went straight into the gym, the physiotherapist was there. He checked all my muscles before I went onto any of the exercise machines. The manager came in and we had a team talk and he told us the line up. I was in the starting line up, I play centre mid. He told us to get back and work out.

It was 1 o'clock and we all went and got a sensible lunch. We went back to the stadium at 2 o'clock. We got our strip on and put our training tops over it. It was 2.30pm and both teams went out to train. Celtic looked very good, their best player was Henrik Larsson. At 5 to 3 both teams went back in. Both teams came out for kick off.

39 minutes into the game Celtic score with a penalty, Henrik Larsson scored it, it was half time, our goal keeper was injured so we had to bring on a sub. 80 minutes, we scored, 2 minutes later, I scored 2-1.

Allan McColgan (12)
Stanley Primary School

A Day In The Life Of A Bird Of Prey

In the morning, the first thing I do is search for food. I go down to the fields where there are lots of mice and small birds. I swoop down and grab it with my talons. Sometimes people try to shoot us for our feathers or for stuffed animals in museums so I have to be careful when I'm flying.

Then I go back to my nest on the cliff face to eat my food. I sometimes go and fly over the mountains for a while. I must always make sure that my mate is looking after the young or another bird might eat them.

I bring more food for the family and some feathers and things to make the nest warm. I have much better eyesight than humans and I can see a rabbit on the ground two miles away. There is another bird in my territory and I will fight it. I use my sharp talons to kill it. My territory is two miles across and usually I fight any other bird that comes in. It is dinner time now and I go to find more food. I see a rabbit on the ground but it escapes so I catch a couple of field mice instead. I take the food back to the nest on the cliff face and settle down to sleep. An eagle's day can be very exhausting.

Alison Macleod (12)
Stanley Primary School

A Day In The Life Of A Rubber

One morning I woke up and I was a rubber. It only lasted a day. Thank goodness because I hated it. I was walking to school. Well trying to. Some boy in my class nearly stood on me.

The bell rang, I went to walk in the door, but it was shut. How would I get in? I walked to the front door. One of the teachers was late so I got in OK. It took me ages to get to my class. Finally I got into class. I try to explain to the teacher why I was late but nobody could hear me. I walked to my desk and climbed up my chair. The person that sat next to me put her hand out to grab me. She rubbed my foot off. She gave me to the teacher to see who I belonged to.

She threw me into a tub which had sharpenings, pins and rulers in it. I fell asleep for the rest of school. The bell woke me up. I climbed out of the tub, walked along the teacher's table, jumped onto her chair, then on to the floor. I got out of school and ran home. When I got home, I wrote a note saying that I would be in very late. I went to the park. My friends came. They didn't notice me, I started to walk home, I got through the cat flap and went to my room. I climbed up my bed and as soon as I put my head on the pillow, I was a human again.

Susan Davidson (11)
Stanley Primary School

A Day In The Life Of A Brain!

Wow! That's me now. Lisa Hunter just woke up at 8.00. I'll be used at 9.00. I'll be used in the morning for sums and afternoon for language. I sometimes have a sore head because I'm always being used.

You know I'm nearly 17. At last Lisa is leaving school because she's 17 but I'm going to sleep now that Lisa is.

I guess I'll be having a longer sleep because I think it's Saturday tomorrow. Hooray. Why did I have to be a brain?

Samantha Gordon (11)
Stanley Primary School

A Day In The Life Of A Film Star

It all started one night before I went to sleep. I started feeling a bit strange. I thought it was just a normal day but when I woke up the next morning and went outside, there were lots of people there taking photographs of me and there was a big black limo waiting for me. I didn't know where we were going so I just went along with it. The limo took me to a television studio and they made me do a film shoot. The film was James Bond. It was very scary and I didn't know what to do in the film.

After the rehearsal, it was taped, then soon after that, they took me outside and people were asking me for my autograph so I gave them it.

Then the limo took me back home, I went up to my room and looked in the mirror and what a sight I saw. I went to sleep. The next morning I was me again, I liked being a film star for a day but it was scary!

Lyndsay Schlesiger (12)
Stanley Primary School

A Day In The Life Of A £5 Note

I am in my mum's purse for 4 hours until my mum takes me out and gives me to Marti for pocket money. He goes to the Pokémon shop but drops me. When he realises what has happened, he goes back to find me but a girl named Stacey picks me up. She goes to International and buys a bobble and T-shirt that says *Don't judge a girl by her T-shirt!* I am in a till until the shopkeeper takes me out and gives me to a girl called Lisa. She goes home and gives me to her brother Mark, who goes to Comet to buy a hi-fi. Marti goes to Comet to buy a television and for change I come out. He gives it to charity who transports me to Africa for the homeless and I saw all these poor children dying.

I'm given to a food shop to buy food for the homeless, I'm then in a till again. Another man comes and takes me to give to his wife for petrol. I'm in a petrol station so a girl gets me as change and she rips me up. My life is over!

Rhona Gracey (10)
Stanley Primary School

A Day In The Life Of A Piece Of Bubblegum

One day I was just sitting on the shelf minding my own business when some child came and picked me up and bought me, then put me in her mouth, chew, chew, chew.

I would think that her jaws would be sore by now. 'Uh oh' they are, here I go getting spat out. 'Ugh too' that's me out, sitting on the ground, a few minutes later somebody stands on me and I am stuck to their shoe. But now he knows I'm there and he has wiped me off and then all of a sudden, I have been picked up by 'Ugh' his breath smells disgusting.

'Oh no' I'm going down his throat, what an exciting life sitting in a dog's stomach, 'Yippee' I think he is trying to cough me out. Yeah, I stink of dog's breath, but at least I'm out.

'Gadz' a little kid has found me and she is scraping me off the ground and is eating me, disgusting but I'm covered in stones so she has spat me back out at the beach into the water. I'm sailing into the middle of the sea. Now a fish has eaten me, I hate being a piece of bubblegum.

Caroline White (11)
Stanley Primary School

A Day In The Life Of Me - A Penny

I was in a till in the Pallazo when a young boy walked in. His sweets came to 49p so the lady handed him over a penny and the penny was . . . me.

When he put me into his pocket, his hands were all sticky. Yuck! They were all dirty. When he was walking home he reached into his pocket to get a tissue and I came out with it.

I was still lying on the pavement an hour later, two men were walking past and one of them picked me up and flung me behind his back. I banged off a shelter, then landed on the grass next to another penny. This one was a shiny one and I was all dirty and sticky.

A lady walked by and picked up the shiny one and left me there. I heard the clock on a tower chime 6 times, so it was 6 o'clock. A little girl walked by and picked me up. When I got to her house, she put me in a jar. A little boy walked into the room, I recognised his face, it was the boy who bought sweets for 49p. He opened the jar and pulled out a handful of pennies. Guess what? I was one of them. Cringe! Back into his pocket I went. He started to fling us, he flung me and I fell down a drain. I went with the flow of the water and ended up washed ashore.

Samantha Anderson (12)
Stanley Primary School

A Day In The Life Of Marshall Mathers

He's sleeping and his daughter Hayley wakes him up wanting a sweetie at 7 o'clock in the morning. Marshall gets up and goes to the shop and gets her a Galaxy Caramel.

When they get home, they watch MTV and Slim Shady's song comes on and he sings it. About an hour later, his wife Kim comes down. Eminem gives her a kiss and she makes breakfast.

After breakfast Marshall receives a phone call from his agent, wanting him to make a new album. He agrees and says he will be there at 1 o'clock. Then he gets another phone call, this time it's Dr Dre. He wants Slim to help him by being in his song. He says he'll be there at 10.30am.

At 10.30 he gives Hayley and Kim a kiss and sets off. He gets held up because everybody wants his autograph. He signs a few and runs as fast as he can. He gets to Dr Dre's house at 11. They work on a song.

Marshall looks at the clock. It's 12.45. He tells Dre he has to go. He leaves and goes to the studios. His agent is there and they work on the album. They call it 'Slim Shady'.

The album has 21 songs on it. He takes a copy home, Kim enjoys it. They go to the park with Hayley, then they go for dinner. After dinner, they order two videos.

You probably want to know how his album got on. His album reached number one on the charts. That's why they call him Slim Shady!

Ryan Harvie (11)
Stanley Primary School

A Day In The Life Of My Dog Hogan

I have had Hogan for eight years and I got him when I was three. He barks when someone is at the door and at night if someone is outside the back door, he growls and sometimes barks.

When I was little and we just got him, me and my family trained him to sit down, roll over, to lie down and do other things. When I was seven I wasn't supposed to train him to jump but one day I went outside with Hogan and trained him to jump gates, fences and walls.

Most of the time we play football outside the back door. When he gets the ball, he kicks it and puts the ball in his mouth so he can run with it. I don't get it but he gets it some way because he puts the ball in his mouth and runs with it, sometimes into the house, or up in the back garden in a corner so I can't get it.

Hogan doesn't bite. He only fights over a female dog that he likes. About two or three years ago Hogan had a girlfriend and she had babies but a year later, Hogan's girlfriend and his puppy were ran down by a car or a bus. The puppy's name was Cain and the mum was Sasha. Hogan ran away but my mum and brother found him, I was happy.

Bradley Hall (11)
Stanley Primary School

A Day In The Life Of A 20p

I went from a lady's pocket called Amy. Then I was in the till for ages. It was really boring and then I went into a little boy's pocket but he did not want me, so he chucked me down the drain and I went down to the sewers.

It was really smelly but when I got to the beach, I lay there for one hour and a little girl picked me up. She bought something and I was in the till again and after that I was in the puggy machine and I was there for the rest of the day.

Nadine Ballantyne (12)
Stanley Primary School

A Day In The Life Of A Clock

Tick, tick, tick, that's what it's like all day. It never stops, oh well I guess that's what I get for wanting to be a clock. Oops better be quiet or Jane and Paul will hear me. Jane and Paul are the children who play in this nursery. Their mum is out all day but the childminder looks after them. The childminder is called Susan Baxter, she is very nice. One day she took Jane and Paul to the fair but when they came back, I had stopped. My batteries had run out.

When Jane and Paul came up to play, they looked at me and said to each other, 'The clock has stopped.'

They both started to cry. Susan who was sitting downstairs heard Jane and Paul crying so she ran upstairs and asked what all the crying was about. Jane told her all about it and then Susan looked up and said that it was only the batteries that had run out. Susan went to buy new batteries for me and I have been working ever since.

Janey Alexander (11)
Stanley Primary School

A Day In The Life Of Freddie The Bus Driver

Every morning when I got on the bus, it was the same bus driver. He was called Freddie. Then one day I went on the exact same bus but Freddie wasn't there, I thought he had died and all sorts of things were going through my mind. Then I saw him coming along the street, 'Phew, I thought you were dead or something. I am so glad you're alive.'

'I am only having a holiday,' he said.

That day he asked me to go to his house for tea and I said I would love to. So I went home with Freddie and I met his wife and children. He had a little boy and girl. They looked lovely. I had a wonderful dinner, I had mince and tatties. They had a beautiful house and garden.

I realised that a bus driver is just the same as normal people, I thought he had a big fancy house and loads of money and a big fancy car. Then I went home and I was telling everybody about it.

The next day I went on the bus but he wasn't there. I asked the bus driver where Freddie was, he said that he had had a heart attack and died earlier that morning.

Sharleen McKinney (11)
Stanley Primary School

A Day In The Life Of My Rabbit

Cuddles woke up about half-past six and went for a drink of water. I went out to see him. Cuddles tried to jump out of his hutch, so I thought he might want to get out. He turned through to the other side, so I closed the hutch door.

At nine o'clock my dad said that I should let Cuddles out. I opened his hutch door and he hopped through. When I put his ramp up, he jumped down and ran about the garden like a dafty. Then he stopped in the shade and started to dig a small hole in the ground and lay down to have a rest. When my little sister came out, he sat up and started running about the garden like a dafty once again. He eventually stopped and ate some heathers in the garden.

At lunchtime, Graeme came round. Cuddles jumped at the sound of the gate banging shut. My mum and dad were sitting out the back, so Graeme joined them. My mum was sitting in the middle of my dad and Graeme. Suddenly, Graeme had felt something rubbing on his leg (he thought it was my mum). When he looked, Cuddles was rubbing his small face on Graeme's leg. Cuddles continued to do this for the next five minutes, but Graeme clapped his hands to make Cuddles go away. It worked. Cuddles ran away to eat the heathers again.

When Graeme left, Cuddles was drinking his water. I was in the house seeing where Lauren was. When I came back out, Cuddles was running about the garden with a cat chasing him. I ran up the back and made a very loud noise and the cat ran away. I checked Cuddles over and luckily, he was fine.

Cuddles was so scared, he hopped up his ramp and into his house. He was lying on his hay sleeping. I quietly closed his hutch. I saw him half an hour later getting a drink of water. He went back through to his hay and fell asleep, preparing for another day.

Heather Boyle (11)
Stanley Primary School

A Day In The Life Of Fred Durst

When he got up he realised the time. It was seven o'clock. He was going to be late for a concert! He got ready and in a flash he was ready for the concert. 'Another close one!' he said.

Once he was ready he got into his car and started to drive to the concert. On his way to the concert he started to sing along to one of his songs that was on a tape. Suddenly the tape started going odd. He stopped the tape and took it out of the tape player. All the stuff had come out of the tape! 'That's the third tape wasted!' he said.

After about two hours he got to his gig. 'Finally, I thought I would never get here!' he said.
He was going to perform in front of 30,000 people. That was OK because he had not performed a lot before this concert. He was going to be singing eleven songs.

After having a look around the stage he decided to go into the cafe and wait for his supporting act. He had not been told who his supporting act was. 'I hope it's not Eminem.'
At that very second the supporting act came in.
'Oh no, it's Eminem!'
Eminem went into the cafe and he found Fred.
'How you doing Lose . . . I mean Eminem!'
'I'm fine, you?'
'I'm fine as well.'

Tonight Fred was about to do his biggest concert and he didn't like his supporting act! Maybe the fans will like him.

Mark Glen (11)
Stanley Primary School

A DAY IN THE LIFE OF MY MUM

In the morning she gets up and gets ready for work. When she goes she shouts, 'Bye,' and goes for the bus.

She doesn't actually go for the bus, she flies to work! It takes her less time and she can save people on her way. My mum had good hearing so if anyone around the world is in danger she goes and saves them. One woman in Poland was in hysterics when my mum saved her.
She said, 'Thanks . . . thanks for saving me, I really appreciate it.'
'No problem,' my mum says. 'It's all in a morning's work.'

No matter how many people she saves my mum always gets to work on time. When she steps in the door she begins to make the children's breakfast (she works in Kerlaw).

At eight o'clock her friend Marion comes in and helps my mum. As soon as breakfast is ready they call the units to get their breakfast. When she goes to the toilet she goes and saves more people. This time it is the President of the United States of America. The White House was burning down so my mum went and put out the fire. The President was saved and everyone was cheering. The President gave her a hero's medal.

After lunch was finished, they went on their lunch break and my mum saved millions of people including Britney Spears and lots of other famous people. They gave my mum lots of signed things for me.

When she comes home she is tired and wants a bath and to relax for a while. My mum is a super mum and I love her.

Kirsty McCubbin (11)
Stanley Primary School

My Invisible Day

One night when I was in my bed as a normal person I woke up at school and I was invisible. I couldn't believe it.

This special kind of make-up I had put on the night before had made me invisible. I couldn't believe it actually worked. I knew I looked different because I looked in the mirror and I couldn't see myself. I was absolutely gobsmacked.

In the morning I went to school and I threw rubbers, pencils and pencil cases at lots of people. In the afternoon I stole the teacher's timetable so she didn't know what to do. At night-time I scared Mum and Dad. They got really frightened because they heard the word, 'Boo!' They got really frightened, scared and really scared to go to bed. The sad thing was it was only a dream. I enjoyed it because it was fun. I would have liked to be a pop star. That would have been absolutely great fun. I'd get to sing, dance and go on tour and do interviews with TV presenters and go out with friends and invite my family around for dinner at my house. I could go out with my pop group and always go to the recording studio.

Nicola McKenzie (9)
Stenhousemuir Primary School

A Day In The Life Of My Teacher

One night I went to bed and the next morning I woke up in a room that wasn't mine. The room had a double bed. I had blue pyjamas on. The bed covers were yellow. The wallpaper was green and violet.

I put on my clothes and saw a blue thing hanging from my top. It said: Miss Ritchie, primary school teacher.

I thought to myself I can't be a teacher, I'm only nine years old. But then I looked in the mirror and I was grown up.

That morning I got my breakfast and went to teach. I did not know what I was doing or saying, so I told a lie. I told the class I had to go somewhere for the afternoon.

That night I went to bed at 1 o'clock in the morning and when I woke up again I was my old self.

Caitlin Robb (9)
Stenhousemuir Primary School

A Day In The Life Of A Dog

Last Friday morning when I woke up I wasn't in my own bed, I wasn't even a human. I was in a kennel in the back garden shivering in the cold wind and the heavy rain. The sun hadn't risen yet and in the sky all I could see were dull grey clouds with rain pouring out of them. Just then I heard someone whistle and shout, 'Here boy.'
I ran to the back door and inside I saw a family of three people. There was a small boy and his mum and dad. The dad gave me some dog biscuits and dried my paws.

Then I noticed that the boy who had to be at least two years younger than me was taller than me. I must have changed into something else apart from a human. I looked down at myself to see and I saw white fur with black spots, four paws and a tail. I was a dalmation dog, which would explain why I was in a kennel.

Since I was a dog I decided to try and act like one, which wasn't going to be easy. I scratched on the door a lot when I wanted to go out to play. When I got out I chased birds, fetched sticks and balls and lay in the shade of my kennel. I did all this until lunchtime when I had one bowl of biscuits and one bowl of meat. After lunch I stayed inside to play with Jack, the little boy until dinner time. For dinner I had the same as I had for lunch. After dinner I watched TV with John the dad. We watched wrestling until 7.30pm and football until 10pm.

Now it was time for bed. I had enjoyed being a dog and wanted to stay that way, but I knew when I woke up in the morning I'd be human and in my own bed again, so one day as a dog would have to do for me.

Robbie Blair (9)
Stenhousemuir Primary School

A Day In The Life Of An Invisible Man

One Friday morning I walked out of my room as usual. I walked to the bathroom to brush my teeth. I looked in the mirror, I had no reflection! I ran downstairs into the living room. I shouted. 'Mum!' It seemed that nobody could hear me. 'I could have fun and games with this.' I giggled.

I went off to school, tripping people up. I got a rope and wrapped it round someone's legs and arms and walked off to school. When I got into school I threw a rubber and hit the teacher on the head.

It was play time, so when I went inside I took the football and ran down the pitch and scored. It was an excellent goal, it hit the top left bar. We went back inside, everybody was talking about my goal. Then we went to do handwriting and I wrote on the board: The teacher is stupid and handwriting is boring. Everything was silent for a minute then the bell rang.

I was walking home and I tripped a few people up. I got in and felt alone. I went to bed and couldn't stop crying. I wanted to be myself again. The next morning I woke up. I was myself again. I went downstairs and ran to school. Everybody in school was talking about yesterday but all I said was, 'I wonder how that could have happened?'

Darryl Extance (10)
Stenhousemuir Primary School

My Dream

One night I was sleeping in my bed and I was having a brilliant dream. It was all about me, my friend Jennifer Kitchen and her brother Oliver. They came for me when I hadn't been expecting them so I went out to play with them.

When I was going in for my tea I asked if my friends could stay over for tea and my mum said it was okay. We had pizza and after, ice cream, then we went out again.

Then we heard the phone ringing, it was their mum. She had to work and nobody could look after them, so my mum offered and they stayed over. That night we were whispering to each other and drawing pictures but then we all fell asleep in the middle of a video called Scream 3. It was very scary and Oliver was crying so I had to go and make him feel better. He just cried even more so I gave him a book. Then we went to sleep. In the morning we went through the living room and watched telly. Then we drew gigantic pictures and wrote letters to people, then we had breakfast. We had Frosties and toast. It was fabulous. Then do you know what? It happened the very next day.

Nicole Innes (9)
Stenhousemuir Primary School

A Day In The Life Of Adolf Hitler

My name is Adolf Hitler. I was born in Austria on April 20th 1889. I grew up in Austria in the city of Linz. My mum was called Karla, she spoiled me. I had five brothers and sisters, three of them died. It's me Adolf and my sister Paula who didn't die. My father was called Alios, he was very strict and cruel to me and Paula. My teacher said I was a lazy, rude and disobedient boy but I didn't like her either.

After I left school I refused to get a job and I was able to live off my mother. I hated the idea of regular work and I passed the days sketching and painting, dreaming of becoming a famous artist.

In 1907 I moved to Vienna, the capital of Austria. Twice I tried becoming a student at the Academy of Fine Arts. I was turned down twice because my paintings weren't good enough.

In 1933 I became Chancellor of Germany and then I had an idea to become an overall leader of Germany. In 1938 Germany occupies Austria and I planned to make a world war called World War II.

In 1939 Germany invaded Poland and it was the Nazi Party who were the main party involved in the invasion. In 1933 I also killed 6,000,000 or more Jews. I managed to kill them by putting them in gas chambers. I particularly enjoyed it when I sent my soldiers out to kill millions of Jews in their homes and I told them to wait for them to come out of their hiding places and then they would kill them. In 1945 I got married to Eva Brown and in the same year we both committed suicide.

Caitlin Heggie (11)
Stenhousemuir Primary School

A Day In A Life Of An Ant

One hot sunny day I woke up and I was hot. I noticed a big difference. I was on a brown crispy leaf. I jumped up and looked around. It was the park round the corner from my house. I was in the grass with mud surrounding me and it was silent and scary.

I looked down at myself and I screamed because I was an ant. I had black and brown skin and big black round eyes. I panicked. The worst thing about that was because I was very small and I thought I would have got squashed.

I thought to myself it is about 9 o'clock. So I went to a dustbin and started to eat some crumbs. I thought this was sick. Then I saw a big spider coming towards me, so I quickly climbed up another leaf. I was safe. At lunchtime and dinnertime I went to the bin again and ate crumbs off a roll. Then I went down to the lake and had a drink of water. There was a worm coming along but it looked more like a snake to me, so I hid behind a can. Then quickly when it went by I ran out. I felt really scared.

Then after that long day I got a nice fresh leaf and I cuddled into a piece of mud and went to sleep. When I woke up I didn't want to look in case I was still an ant but I wasn't. I was myself again and the piece of mud was still there so I put it in a tube.

I thought to myself, if I turn into anything again it would be a butterfly. Then I said, 'I had a good day but I wouldn't want to be an ant again.'

Emma Sharp (10)
Stenhousemuir Primary School

A Day In The Life Of A Pop Star

Last Wednesday I woke up ready to go to school but I wasn't in my own room. I was staying at the top of the Empire State Building in New York City and not only that I was Britney Spears the pop star.

I went through to the bathroom and looked at myself. I had a silk night-dress on, pink slippers with little pigs on them and a pink silk night gown on. I was on a different planet totally. I heard a knock at the door.
'Come in,' I said. It was my maid Jill with my breakfast.
'Sausage, egg and bacon with a glass of orange juice, Britney.' Jill said.
'Thanks,' I said.
After I'd finished my breakfast I thought, I have lots of money so I'll go shopping. But I didn't go in a regular car, I went in a limousine. I bought lots of stuff. When I got home I rode my horse called Sparkle. She has won twelve trophies and twelve ribbons. She got a little tired so I brought her in her stable and she had a rest. I was feeling peckish so I had lunch, I had cheese pizza and a freshly picked salad and it was lovely. I was so full I had a sleep myself.

My day was almost over. It was 5pm so I went for a swim with my dolphin Whizz, it was great fun, I had a swim for an hour and after, I went into my bedroom and washed my hair. I put on my purple dress and went out for dinner. I had spaghetti bolognese and garlic bread and it was lovely. I ate every bit and finally I went home and watched TV for a while. I watched my favourite TV show Friends and as my head hit the soft pillow the thoughts of the day melted away.

Hopefully I will wake up and be Charlotte Crawford, because being a pop star is very stressful.

Charlotte Crawford (10)
Stenhousemuir Primary School

My Invisible Day

One morning on the 12th November at 7am I headed for the bathroom to get washed. I walked in and looked in the mirror. I could not see myself. I was gone and then I remembered my dream. I was invisible, so I got ready for school and left my school bag behind.

I am invisible, invisible, invisible, I sang all the way to school. I scared everyone in the class and then I went and got a bucket from the back and filled it up with water and poured it on someone's chair and they got soaked. Then I took someone's school bag and they screamed and put the stuff back down and they got in trouble. Then I tied everyone's laces together and they tripped up.

When I got outside it was a laugh. I threw stones and stole footballs and kicked them away and saved goals. When I got back into the class I went to the people I hated, waited till they went out to ask the teacher something and rubbed out their work and threw their pencil, rubber and sharpener out of the window.

When I was walking home I got struck by lightning. I was back to normal, so I just went home. The next day I had powers but I never used them.

Kelly Webster (9)
Stenhousemuir Primary School

My Dream Come True

One night when I went to bed as a normal person I woke up as a pop star. I knew I had changed because when I went to the bathroom to put my make-up on, I looked in the mirror. The next thing I noticed was that I was in a hotel and that I had long hair instead of short hair.

In the hotel there was a fountain that was squirting perfume out of it. It also had light blue fluffy carpets which were really soft.

When I went out for lunch in an eleven seated car I met ten friends and we all went to a restaurant for lunch. Then after we had had our lunch we went shopping for four hours. We all started to get hungry so seven of them went home for their dinner and the four of us left just went back to the hotel for our dinner.

Then all of a sudden I woke up and realised that it was all a dream, but it was the best dream I've ever had in my whole life.

I enjoyed it so much because I love going shopping and going out for lunch. The best thing was that my dream had come true and I would never have such a good dream as the one I just had.

Tyler Johnston (9)
Stenhousemuir Primary School

A Day In The Life Of Geri Halliwell

I woke up thinking it was a perfectly normal day but when I opened my eyes I saw a glistening, huge chandelier. I knew it wasn't my room. I got out of the double bed with purple quilt covers and had a look around. I saw the biggest floor, the size of three rooms. It had glass tiles and they looked like they had been cleaned five times a day. There was a fountain right in the middle of the room, it was beautiful. I went outside and there was a huge swimming pool with a Jacuzzi next to it. I wandered back in and went into the bathroom, there was a huge bath with an electric shower. The sink was shining with absolutely no dust on it at all. I glanced in the body sized mirror.

I looked exactly like Geri Halliwell, my hair was ginger, sparkling and my pjs had 'Geri' in big bold, gold letters. I also noticed that I was still very skinny (I looked wonderful).
'Miss Halliwell,' shouted the maid, 'your curry is getting cold.'
'I'll be there in a minute,' I called. I walked through to see a beautiful maid with long brown hair and a black dress on. I ate my curry and thanked the maid. I raked all the drawers and found a swimming suit. I put it on and dived into the pool. I swam the whole length of the pool and I got out and got dried with a red towel that looked like it was bought yesterday. I ran down the flight of stairs and a man with a black coat on said, 'Would you like a ride in your limo?'
I said, 'I'd love to.' I switched on the TV and watched Brookside. When we got back I got a kebab pizza for lunch. I called to the maid.
'Have a drink.'
'Thank you,' said the maid. We had a drink together.
I said, 'May I go to Emma's for dinner tonight?'
'Yes,' called the maid.
I hopped in the limo. I said, 'To Emma's please.'
We arrived in about ten minutes. Emma was glad to see me.
'I cooked your favourite, burger and chips,' she said.

‘Thanks,’ I said hungrily. I ate dinner with Emma and after an hour I went home (it was midnight). I went to sleep and I couldn’t wait till morning. I felt brilliant because I was famous and I couldn’t wait till I had to sing ‘It’s Raining Men’.

Nicole West (10)
Stenhousemuir Primary School

A Day In The Life Of A Witch

One morning I woke up in bed and I pointed at the radio. Suddenly it came on. Then I pointed at the cupboard and it opened. I said, 'Cool,' I am a witch.

I had my breakfast and got ready for school. Then I said to myself I am going to start putting spells on people. So first I went to my worst enemy Lisa. I made this boy run through a puddle and soak her. Then I made all her books start flying out of her bag. Suddenly, the bell rang, Lisa was crying because her dress and all her books were wet. Everyone was laughing because she was being a baby. When I got inside I didn't feel like doing any work. So I used my powers to write all over the board.
'I don't want to do any work.'
Then I went to the toilet and made myself invisible. I pulled people's hair, wrote on their jotters and threw things all over the place. At lunchtime I changed myself back and I had my lunch. After I had my lunch I went outside and made the ropes stop that people were playing with. I made the piggy in the middle ball land on the school roof. The bell rang to go back in again so I did the work in the afternoon. A whole two hours of boring work. I used spells to do my work.

At home time I made myself invisible and made myself able to fly so I flew home. I made my dinner disappear and I made lots and lots of my favourite chocolates and sweets come. I ate them all. I got all the latest CDs with my powers and listened to them for hours. Then I pointed at my piggy bank and a whole load of money came out. Then I said to myself, 'I want more,' so I pointed again and even more came out.

Every time I wanted more money I just pointed at my piggy bank and even more came out. I didn't know where it was coming from though. I bought mobile phones, CDs, a Gameboy and a bike. I didn't use my powers to get the things because it was ruining them. I loved having magical powers.

The next day I tried my powers, they still worked. I felt great. It was Saturday. With my magical powers I made myself turn into Britney Spears. I was suddenly at a concert. I was singing 'Stronger'. I had the right singing voice and everything. After the concert I got Britney's handwriting and I signed autographs. Then I changed myself back. I wondered what Britney Spears would have thought being me for a few hours. Britney Spears is my favourite pop star. She would probably like being herself better. I liked being her.

There is one thing I have learnt from all that has happened. Magical powers are great. I wonder what I will do next with my powers?

Ruth Prophet (9)
Stenhousemuir Primary School

A DAY IN THE LIFE OF A LION

One morning I woke up somewhere very strange. It had huge lush green trees and sandy grounds plus long green grass. There were lots of little animals running about. There were buffalo and wildebeest. There were lots and lots of insects.

Then I looked down at myself. I had golden fur, brown and orange mane and brown eyes and a huge mouth. I had a tail and I was on all fours. I was a lion, yes, I was a lion.

Next morning I was hungry, so for breakfast I killed a Thompson gazelle. It was yuck and horrible and even stinky. Then I had a big, big snooze under the sun. I loved it, it was excellent. For lunch I had a buffalo. It was all right but it wasn't brilliant. In the afternoon I hung out with other lions and it was great. We killed lots of little animals and we started play fighting. For dinner I ate a zebra, it was all right and in the evening I had a big snooze.

Next morning I was walking about and I saw a tiger. It ran over to me and pounced on me and killed me. Then I woke up and I realised it was the end of my day. I enjoyed my day very much, it was great.

Cameron Moore (8)
Stenhousemuir Primary School

A Day Of Being Kym

I went to bed on the Friday at 11.00pm and woke up on the Saturday at 9am in a big posh room. It had a king size bed. In the bathroom there was a toilet, big bath, sink and Jacuzzi. In where the bed was there were two veranda doors that opened and took you to a big pool and a bar.

I looked like Kym out of Hear'say. I had brown eyes and brown hair with red streaks through it. I have changed because I had a dream and it came true. I know I look different because I looked in the mirror.

In the morning I had breakfast then went to the studio to do some of my video.

I went to bed on the Saturday and woke up on the Sunday and I was me again. I had my own clothes and I was in my own bed.

Kasha Pow (9)
Stenhousemuir Primary School

A Day in The Life Of . . . Kym From Popstars

One morning I woke up and it was quite strange. My dad always calls for breakfast. I was not wide awake and it was all blurred. It looked like a glass roof in the middle of New York. I'm probably just dreaming, I thought. So I shook my head and walked into the bathroom. I looked in the mirror . . .

Aaaagh . . . It was not me I was looking at but Kym from Popstars! Then I spoke, 'What? What? What?' It can't be. I always wished I could be Kym. I went back to bed and a lady came in with a tray with bacon, egg and sausages, *mmmm.*
'Can I get you anything else mam?'
'No thank you,' I said.
Hey wait a minute, I actually speak like Kym too. The maid started to rake through my wardrobe which was now full of wonderful clothes. Then all my worries went away.

Then I went for a bath but it was not there. In its place was a Jacuzzi and a door marked sauna and beside me another marked, 'private swimming pool and shower'. I went in. There was a swimming pool and shower, it was great, so I had a swim then a shower then I got ready. I had a leather skirt and sequinned top! Wow! Then I walked out of my door there was a sign marked 'Kym, Popstars'.

This was absolutely great! I went to reception and the man gave me a timetable marked 'breakfast, morning press conference 9 o'clock'.

There was a limousine waiting outside and a man helped me in. There, in the car was a private phone, pizza, champagne and a sunroof, cool! I was very excited and when we pulled over I was in front of a building which was white which looked brown inside because only I could see out. When I got out I went into the building I went up in three lifts then six corridors and then nine staircases! Finally, I got to a room and went in. I was greeted by Danny, Suzanne, Noel and Myleene.
'Hey guys, how are you?'
'Fine,' said Suzanne, 'we have our concert tonight, it will be great!'

Oh no, but when I started to sing I sounded just like Kym! I went into the hall and everyone was looking at me and I was really embarrassed but it was okay. I know what to say because I knew so much about Kym. After that I went back to my hotel and Danny said, 'Remember the interview at the radio station.'
'Yeah!' I said in a shaky voice.
I went out in the afternoon again and went to an interview. It was hard work but it was good as well. I looked at my timetable - go out with mates (Suzanne and Myleene). So I went out, got a fancy meal, got wine and champagne, then I went to the hotel again and got a snack. I was going to bring my bag to the concert and costume. I went in a limousine again. I went to a dressing room and I went on stage and I sang all the songs and I was so excited I nearly screamed! It was great because everyone was watching me and the lights were great. After that I went back and got supper. After that I went out and it was lightning. I got struck by lightning and I was back to my old self again! I was in my pyjamas and I then thought what a great day . . . amazing.

Hannah Prophet (9)
Stenhousemuir Primary School

A Day In The Life Of Roald Dahl

My name is Roald Dahl. I was born in 1916 in Wales. I have Norwegian parents. I was educated in England. My first job was working for Shell oil company in Africa. I began writing after I quit my oil job, it went out of business. I felt like I needed to write every day, but then I was called to be a fighter pilot and I am here on my first day.

I am petrified, I have just woken up. It is five o'clock in the morning. I have to get ready quickly, so I am there for our plane's attack on the Germans. In two hours and ten minutes we will be fighting for England. Now I am shivering with fear as I am thinking of it. My teeth are chattering and I cannot help it. I am dreading the battle but know the time has come to start fighting for England.

I have just started fighting, the hairs on my neck are standing on end. I have a companion with me. He is just as nervous. It is really tough, I have just been hit.

I am badly hurt, I am going back to land. Now I feel faint. I have got a bash on the head, it really hurts. I have got a thumping headache. I have thought of my title because I have already wrote it. I will call it 'The BFG', it stands for 'big friendly giant'.

I died in 1990 at the age of 74, these are some of the books I wrote: James And The Giant Peach, Charlie And The Chocolate Factory, The Magic Finger, Charlie And The Great Glass Elevator, Fantastic Mr Fox, Matilda, The Twits, The BFG and The Witches. I am the most well known writer for children's books.

Laura Barry (10)
Stenhousemuir Primary School

A Day In The Life Of Queen Victoria

My name is Alexandrina Victoria. I was born on the 24th May 1819, in Kensington Palace in London. My mother is Victoria Mary Louisa and my father is Edward Augustus, Duke of Kent and Strathern.

One day when I was eighteen, I was sitting in front of my mirror. I heard a knock at my door and when I opened it I saw two men standing talking. They came in and kissed me. They said 'We have come to tell you that you are the new Queen of England, due to William IV's death.' I was really delighted but really didn't like the thought of William IV being dead.

Three years later I married a prince called Albert, Prince of Saxe-Coburg-Gotha, who I had known for about four years. I had nine children. My first of the nine was Victoria Adelaide Mary Louise, later Empress of Germany. My first son was Albert Edward, Prince of Wales and later, King of Great Britain. I later had 40 grandchildren whom nearly all of them were married into royal families. I reigned for 64 years, from 1837-1901.

Who would have ever thought that I was the longest serving Queen for England!

Garry McInnes (10)
Stenhousemuir Primary School

A Day In The Life Of Florence Nightingale

My name is Florence Nightingale. I was born on the 12th May 1820 in Florence (Italy). When I was sixteen I thought I heard the voice of God. I believe he was calling me to do special work. I did not tell anyone. I waited nearly two years before I knew what God wanted me to do. I decided to help the poor, hungry and sick people. My parents were angry. I was determined anyway. I got up early every morning to study medicine in secret. Then when I was twenty-seven my family sent me to Rome. There I met Sidney Herbert, he introduced me to others who felt the same. I returned more determined than ever. I convinced my parents to let me go to Kaiserwerth Institution for three years. When I returned home my sister, father and grandmother were ill. Instead of working in a hospital I cared for my family. The next year, I took a job for caring for gentlewomen. My mother was horrified but my father supported me. He gave me £500 per year to live on.

The next year I offered to care for people suffering from Cholera. It was hard but I didn't care. (My old friend Sidney Herbert is now a member of the Government.) The Crimean War had started, it was very chaotic in hospitals so I wrote to Sidney Herbert. I offered my help. He wrote back and asked me to gather a group of nurses to go to the Crimea. (This was the first time a woman had been asked to do such an important job.) It was extremely difficult for me to find good, trained nurses but I finally managed to get a group of thirty-eight women. I ordered supplies and I was sent some by the readers of 'The Times'. When we arrived at the hospital in Scutari in Turkey we were appalled by what we saw. The hospital was filthy, the drains were blocked. The injured lay on the floor, covered in filthy, bloody rags. There were rats and fleas everywhere, there was little food. Worst of all, the army doctors were not pleased to see us. They would not let us nurse the sick and wounded. So I set my nurses to checking stores and sewing. They did not have to wait long. Not long after we arrived the wounded started to pour in. The army doctors were overwhelmed and at last asked my nurses and I to help. I instructed my nurses to work cleaning the hospital. I asked local people to help unblock the drains and I used the money I had received from 'The Times' to buy food and medical supplies.

In just a few weeks we had cleaned up the hospital wonderfully, we had improved conditions and as a result the death rate fell from 45 percent to 2 percent. I often worked twenty-four hours a day. The soldiers called me 'The Lady with the Lamp' because every night I walked around the wards to look after the sick.

By the time the war ended in 1856, I was a national heroine.

Jennifer Graham (10)
Stenhousemuir Primary School

A Day In The Life Of Princess Diana

My name is Princess Diana. I was born in Park House on July 1st 1961. My mother is Frances Shand Kydd. My stepfather is Peter Shand Kydd. My mother-in-law is Queen Elizabeth. I have two sons, Prince William my eldest son and Prince Harry.

I looked out my bedroom window. I was amazed to see so many people. I was leaving to go to Luton airport. As I walked out the palace, a picture flashed in my eyes. I felt so unsafe with people taking photos of me. As the guards opened the gate I walked through, not knowing what to expect. As I got to the other side of the gate I heard people shouting and pointing at me. As I walked along the red carpet people were giving me roses, flags, flowers and all sorts of things. I was shaking people's hands all the way to the car. As I got in the car I saw lots of camera flashes. I started to feel safer away from the palace. As I watched all the sights pass I felt happy and very lucky to live in this beautiful city.

As I arrived at the airport there were more crowds. I asked the driver to drive me round the back of the airport so no one would crowd me. As I walked up the stairs to leave for Angola, I looked at my city before I went into my seat.

I walked off the plane in this very hot country. I walked through an alleyway and an old lady held on to my feet. I bent over, touched her head and gave her bread and corn. I settled in my hotel for the night. I had a big day ahead of me.

The next morning I set off to the minefield. I walked through the minefield and then spoke to the people that had been injured in the minefield. I felt like I could cry when people told me the stories about their lives. After hearing all of the people's stories I felt really bad. A little boy came and gave me an Angolan flag. I held many children's hands and spoke to other people. As I drove to the airport I thought about what I had done.

After about four hours I arrived back at the palace. I felt glad to see my family again and thankful that I had helped all these people.

Gordon Campbell (11)
Stenhousemuir Primary School

A DAY IN THE LIFE OF FLORENCE NIGHTINGALE

My name is Florence Nightingale. I was born in a city called Florence in 1820. My mum told me that she called me Florence because of its beauty and also because we lived there. But in those days it was very unusual to call someone after a city. I was born into a rich English family. My mum and dad thought I would grow up and meet a rich husband, who would look after me and care for me. But it wasn't to be, I had other ideas on my mind. When I was about 16 years old I believed that God had spoken to me, telling me to do special work. I knew not to say anything of this because everyone would think I am crazy and lock me up. Not long after this, me and my family went on a tour through Europe for about two years. But I still believed that God wanted me to do something special.

It took me two years to decide what God wanted me to do. That was to help the poor, hungry and sick people. But where was I to start? When I asked my parents if I could learn to be a nurse, they were totally furious and shocked. I didn't care what my mum and dad said!

The Crimean war broke out in 1854. Britain and France sent soldiers to help the Turks fight the Russians. Just before the war I went to visit some of the hospitals. I went to them and I saw what they were like and every one of the nurses were drunk and more people were dying of shock than their actual injuries. I studied medicine for two years. I was on duty day and night because of the war. I walked around with a lamp and the injured soldiers named me *The lady with the lamp.* It was very gruesome when I had to help a man cut off someone's leg when he was awake.

As soon as the war was over I went to talk to Queen Victoria. She talked about how to change hospitals and improve army hospitals. A health department was set up in India because of my care for the poor people.

I set up a nursing training school. When I was about 89 I started writing books about nursing. All hospitals are clean and healthy now and no one is drunk. That is why I am known as *The lady with the lamp.*

Nicola Aitken (10)
Stenhousemuir Primary School

Invisible Me

A year ago now, I was in my bed and I woke up and as usual I was lying in my bed.

I got up and brushed my hair and looked in the mirror. I looked perf . . . I . . . I . . . looked like . . . erm . . . nothing. I wasn't there. I was sure I was standing in front of the mirror because I could see it right in front of me. I just wasn't there. Then it struck me like a bolt of lightning. I was invisible. I thought for a minute, this could be fun.

I got up quickly and got dressed even though I could have just kept my PJs on, but I didn't want to take the risk. Then I was dressed. I thought, where could I cause havoc this morning. Then I thought, I'll go to school. As per usual I was late but it didn't really matter. When I got inside the school I went to my classroom. My teacher, Miss Harley had wrote a lot of stuff on the blackboard, so I got the duster and wiped it all off.

When the teacher came in after the children, Miss Harley was about to blow her last gasket when she said in her normal, sweet voice, 'Who wiped the stuff on the board off?'
There was a pause. No one came forth so the whole class got into trouble. When they all sat down I knocked all their pencil cases off the tables and again they all got into trouble. Soon it was lunch time and I stayed for lunch at school. I knocked all the students' lunches off the tables. After, when everyone came in smelling of curry or mushroom soup, Miss Harley had to open every window in the room. But I wasn't finished, oh no, the best trick was about to begin.

I hated this girl in my class called Lily, so I took her very expensive new pencil case and threw it at the teacher.
Miss Harley said, 'Lily,' and just then the bell rang. Miss Harley asked Lily to stay and explain why her pencil case was on the floor. Lily was told to clap the dusters for a week for her punishment. When Lily got out the room I took her new, pink, fluffy hat and threw it in the mud outside.

When I got home I didn't eat my tea, I just pretended there was a ghost in the house by making 'ooohh' noises and moving stuff around. I yawned and thought I'd better go to bed now and as my head touched the pillow I turned back to normal. I thought, wow, and as I slept, I thought this had been the best day in my whole life.

Sarah Trotter (10)
Stenhousemuir Primary School

The Witchy Day!

One night I was dreaming of being a witch. A witch that is so powerful to rule the world. Then I woke up and in surprise I found myself in a dark, gloomy, dusty castle. I thought, this is just like my dream. There were tables and chairs knocked over, cauldrons and books and even broomsticks in the cupboards.

There was an old cracked mirror on the wall. I looked in it and I saw I had changed from a young girl to an old, ugly, grey-haired witch. I thought, this really must be from my dream!

Suddenly a rather strange looking gnome came in the room with a tray of bowls filled with green, slimy, gooey soup. He gave me one whilst staring at me almost as if he had never seen anyone so ugly before. First I ate the soup and then I decided to read one of the books, so I did. Soon after the little gnome appeared again with more soup. He gave me some and off he went again. I decided to try one of the spells from the book and when I did, poof! Me and the little gnome were invisible. In a school the little gnome started playing tricks on people so I joined in too. We tied shoelaces together and threw things at people until the spell wore off and we were back in the castle. We agreed it was fun when we were having more soup for dinner. When it got to the part when I was alone in the room reading, I woke up and that was the end of a witchy day!

Kirstie MacMorran (10)
Stenhousemuir Primary School

A DAY IN THE LIFE OF ANNE FRANK

Dear Kitty,
I was born on the 12th June 1929 in Frankfurt-am-Main in Germany. Later we moved to Amsterdam. This diary was a birthday present for my 13th birthday. I live with my father, mother and sister Margot. I was called Annielies Marie, Anne for short. I have many friends and I also have a cat. But now I've had to give all this up and move into a secret annexe above the office where my father works.

Today my father told me that we would have to move into a secret annexe above the office where he worked. I would have to leave behind all my friends and our cat to live there. We couldn't go out into the streets carrying a suitcase. I wore two vests, three pairs of pants, a dress, and over that a skirt, a jacket, a raincoat, two pairs of stockings, heavy shoes, a cap, a scarf, and lots more. I was suffocating before we left. When we went to the annexe, all day long we unpacked boxes, filled cupboards, hammered nails and tidied up the mess until we fell exhausted into our clean beds. Later on we were joined by the van Daans and doctor Albert Dussel. I soon fell in love with their son Peter van Daan. At night I would cuddle into my father because of the screams and gunshots.

Some day I hope my diary will be published for other people to read. They will learn of all the suffering and death caused by the war and of all the Jews that were killed during the Holocaust.

Louise Bell (11)
Stenhousemuir Primary School

A Day In The Life Of Florence Nightingale

My name is Florence Nightingale. I was born on May 12th 1820 in Florence. I was named after my birthplace.

In 1846 a friend of mine sent me to the Year Book of the Institution of Protestant Deaconesses at Kaisersworth in Germany which trained girls to nurse the sick. Four years later I entered the institution and went through the full course of training as a nurse. In 1853 I got picked to nurse in Gentlewomen in London.

The Crimean war broke out in March 1854. I volunteered to leave in three days to help the soldiers who were injured. I took three nurses with me to Constantinople. I was in charge of the military hospitals in Turkey.

The hospital was damp, dark and creepy because it was wrecked during the battle. After the battle of Inkerman the hospital was crowded with injured soldiers. It was a messy and bloody sight. There were men lying everywhere. There was no clothing or bedding. All the supplies had broken down, but I had authority to purchase outside the hospital. I had brought £30,000 with me. I spent tiring hours in the hospital. Each night I made my rounds giving comfort and advice and establishing the wounded soldiers' conception of 'the lady with the lamp'.

I became ill with a fever. Shortly after the last patient left the barrack hospital I sailed for England. I returned home. I had a long interview with Queen Victoria, the Prince Consort and Lord Panmure, Herbert's successor. I worked in lots of other hospitals.

I got old. My eyesight gradually failed, until in 1901 I became completely blind. I died in 1910. My wish was to be buried in Westminster Abbey.

Laura Stewart (10)
Stenhousemuir Primary School

A Day In The Life Of William Wallace

'My name is William Wallace. I live at Elderslie near Paisley. I am always remembered for the battle of Stirling Bridge. Before that I was already known to the people of Scotland because of my exploits against the English.

In July 1297 an English army headed for Scotland to crush me and my army. When I heard this I headed for Stirling where I met up with a young knight called Andrew Murray who also had a large army with him. Myself and Murray took position on the Abbey Craig, a small hill overlooking Stirling. When the English appeared in our sight, Murray and I sent our troops to hide behind a narrow path from the bridge. The next day the rest of mine and Murray's troops showed themselves to the English. This brought the English troops over the bridge to meet us in battle. When half the English were over the bridge the Scots that were hiding at the side of the road attacked those rotten English troops. Myself and Murray joined the attack with the remaining. The English could not turn back over the bridge because it was full. We slaughtered them, we chopped off some heads, we slit their necks. Blood was sloshing everywhere! Some of them fell off the bridge and drowned. Blood was dripping off the bridge! A few hours later we won with at least 5000 English dead. Sadly Andrew Murray was wounded. He died two weeks later. I, William Wallace, will go on to clear Scotland of all English troops.'

Andrew Dixon (10)
Stenhousemuir Primary School

A Day In The Life Of John Logie Baird

My name is John Logie Baird. I was born in Helensburgh in the west coast of Scotland in 1888 on the 13th August. My parents were the Reverend John and his wife Jessie. I have two sisters and a brother.

I was never very healthy and I grew up to like science, especially anything to do with electricity. In my days very few people had electric lights or telephones in their homes. When I was a boy, I set up my own telescope exchange in my bedroom. Next, I set up a generator to supply the house with electric light. The generator was made out of all kinds of bits and pieces, including old jam jars. I was also very interested in photography. One of my experiments was to enlarge photos.

After I left school I went to the Royal Glasgow College of Technology. It was around this time that I started thinking about the idea of television. I thought that if sounds could be sent by radio waves, then pictures could too. For most people this was just a dream. My time at college was cut short when the First World War started in 1914. I volunteered at once to fight for my country, but I was turned down because of my poor health.

I soon forgot about my idea for the television but soon after, I remembered about it again. I thought that if I could send a picture from one room to another, why couldn't I send a person. I found William Taynton, sat him in a room with lots of lights. Then I wondered if it had worked . . . and it had. I showed my idea to the Prime Minister and he thought it was brilliant.

In 1922, BBC started broadcasting the first TV programmes. In 1931, I travelled to America and I married Margaret Albu. I started calling the television, a television. In 1937, the BBC chose a rival system that used a completely different method of scanning pictures. It was a blow to me, but did not stop me working on other ideas.

I also helped invent lots of other things. I helped invent the development of radar which is used to help ships and aircraft find their ways. I helped develop the computer mouse. My patents, 'Telecrome', electronic colour television. My super TV set is demonstrated. I myself missed the demonstration due to illness. I died on the 14th June 1946.

Rachel Kirk (10)
Stenhousemuir Primary School

A Day In The Life Of Napoleon

My name is Napoleon Bonaparte. I was born on August 15th 1769 in Ayaccio, Corsica, an island under French rule. My mum's name was Letzia and my dad was called Carlo. In 1778 my father sent me to a French Military Academy at Brienne where I spent the next five years. I later attended the Ecole Militare (military school) in Paris and in 1785 I was commissioned a second lieutenant in artillery. During the next several years I served at various obscure army posts. As I grew up my dream was to conquer all of Europe.

One morning in late March I was woken up at 5.30am. I was given the command to drive the Austrians and the Sardinians out of Italy. I had many brilliant victories and acquired Lombardy, the city of Nice and the duchy of Savoy. This one though, I thought, would be a lot tougher. Then in 1797 the hardest one of all to come. I had to cross the Alps and advance on Vienna. I was really scared. The only thing that was running through my mind was would I make it? It was a hard and long journey. When we reached Vienna in the heart of the night we found the Austrians waiting for us. A battle started. As it raged on, people were dying all about me. It was a sickening sight. It was the hardest battle I had ever been in. I was petrified I'd lose my life.

Eventually the Austrians waved the white flag and called for an Armistice (truce) and were forced to sign the treaty of Campo Formio, which ceded to France the Belgian provinces and other territories. I felt very tired and pleased. I was battered and bruised and had been stabbed from the battle. I also felt very sad because my best friend had been killed. I also felt a great sense of triumph because I had crossed the Alps.

In 1804 I was crowned emperor of France. I never thought that I could conquer as many countries.

Gavin Brown (10)
Stenhousemuir Primary School

A DAY IN THE LIFE OF FLORENCE NIGHTINGALE

My name is Florence Nightingale and when I was working, my nickname was 'Lady of the Lamp'. I was born in May 12th 1820 in Florence. I was an English nurse and the founder of trained nursing as a profession for women.

In 1854-56, during the Crimean War, I was in charge of nursing in the military hospitals at Scutari, in Turkey where I coped with conditions of crowding, inadequate sanitation and shortage of basic necessities. In 1860, I established in London the Nightingale School for nurses, the first in the world.

I was named after my birthplace, meaning it was Florence - Florence Nightingale. I was educated by my father, he taught me six different languages, English, Greek, Latin, French, German and Italian.

The Crimean War broke and millions and millions of soldiers came to see me. I did two horrible things today, I had to hold a man down while a woman cut his leg off and I had to cut a man's arm off. It was a gruesome sight!

Sarah Grant (10)
Stenhousemuir Primary School

A Day In The Life Of Florence Nightingale . . .

My name is Florence Nightingale. I was born in Italy in 1820. I was trained as a nurse at a time when there were very few professional nurses in England. I became involved in the Crimean War when the Russian Grand Duchess Elena Pevlouna founded 'Community of the Cross' organisation to send female assistance to the sick and wounded on the battlefield.

News of the conditions reached England and Sidney Herbert, the secretary of war, sent a passionate plea to the Establishment for Gentle Woman During Illness to introduce female nurses into the military hospitals in Turkey. I was accepted immediately. I arrived in Scutari with thirty-eight nurses and was to change the course of military medicine forever. I felt really nervous.

I found two thousand wounded all lumped together lying packed tight, they were in dirty clothes and linen covered in blood and stained. I wanted to separate them and put them on a bed of their own. They looked very uncomfortable. Men were unshaven and unwashed, some with only their coats as covers.

I became known as the lady with the lamp, when I looked after British soldiers injured in the Crimean war. I visited each patient with my lamp in my hand every night, making sure each soldier was as comfortable as possible.

There were enormous casualties in this war, but I discovered even higher casualties from the filthy barrack hospitals. I introduced one man to one bed, and acted to reform cleaning, laundry, sanitation, water, food and finance policies.

In 1858 I published ‘Notes on Nursing’ in which I talked about ‘household hygiene’. I did much to increase the general awareness of personal hygiene and its effect on health promotion.

I died in 1919 having made nursing a respectable professional career for ladies.

Sara McConnell (10)
Stenhousemuir Primary School

A Day In The Life Of Adolf Hitler

My name is Adolf Hitler. I was born on 20th April, 1889 in Austria.

When I was little, I wanted to be an artist. I left school on 14th June at the age of 16.

In 1903 my father died. After his death, my mother, my seven brothers and sisters and I lived only on my mother's pension.

After my mother's death in 1907, I moved to Munich, Germany and in 1919 I started a group that became known as the Nazi party.

I became the leader of the Nazi party very quickly. Three months later I volunteered to be in the army. Whilst this was happening World War I was being fought.

In 1923 I was imprisoned by my political opponents because the Nazi party tried to take over the government. Whilst I was in prison I wrote a book called Mein Kampf (My Struggle).

When I was released nine months later *I came to power!*

I took over Germany. I hated Jews and so I told my army to kill every Jew they saw. In the end over 6,000,000 Jews were killed.

I ordered death camps to be built, where Jews were told to have a shower. The showers were really gas chambers.

It was because of me and my army that World War II began!

In 1940 Nazi and Germany with their army conquered France, Poland, Belgium, Luxembourg, Denmark and Norway.

By 1944, people had begun to really hate me, but I was obstinate. I would *not* let my chief soldiers decide what was best for Germany, so we lost the war!

Later on in 1944, a bomb was laid in my briefing room. I was very nearly killed. By then, I had lost my trust in my officers and government ministers.

In 1945, I married a woman I'd known for five years. Her name was Eva Braun. She seemed to be the only one I could trust!

Although Germany lost the war, my life changed world history forever!

Laura Johnston (10)
Stenhousemuir Primary School

ROBERT THE BRUCE

'Hello, my name is Robert Bruce. I was born in 1274. Now, here is my life story.

I always wanted to be King of Scotland. Before me there were a few great kings and leaders. From 1296 until 1306 Scotland did not have a king. During this time William Wallace led an uprising and became 'master' of Scotland. Wallace, however, was captured by Edward I and put to death in 1305. Months later I became the great champion of Scotland, and I was crowned King of Scotland in 1306 at Scone.

The battle of Bannockburn

The armies were getting ready. I was armed with soldiers, cavalry and one King. When the armies moved they raced at each other killing some in the first movement. The battle was in full gear. The English had twice as many soldiers. People were slaughtered to their feet. Archers firing arrows. English from the east, Scottish from the west. Everywhere you looked someone was killed. Men beheaded and chopped. We were still in it. Pushing forward we scared them, pushing back they scared us. Then the small folk with their saucepans and kettles scared some English away. 'We want independence,' they said. The battle was nearly finished. The last Englishmen standing ran away like chickens. We had won. *Victory was ours!* We celebrated a triumphant win. This battle ensured Scotland would stay independent of England.'

Ross Kinnaird (11)
Stenhousemuir Primary School

A Day In The Life Of Roald Dahl

Dear Diary,
Can you believe that it was only last year that I was blowing people up from the sky? Oh how I long for those days to come back but I can't change it. I'm getting older. I'll be 27 come June, but I think I look alright for 26, after all, no wrinkles, no grey hairs yet! I'm in the middle of writing my first book. It's called *The Gremlins*. It's about the old stories of little things inside the engines of the RAF's cruisers. It's both funny and scary. My girlfriend and I think it's coming along nicely.

I was called into my boss' office. He almost fired me but I managed to save my job by explaining to him that writing a book was a very hard thing. I mean you have to make sure that it's absolutely perfect. Capital letters, full stops, the works! So he gave me some extra time.
'But if it's not finished in the next ten weeks you're fired,' he shouted.

Here is the best news of all, my book (if it sells well) and I'm really worked up about this, I mean this is the all-time best my book, my very own book is going to be made into a full motion feature film. Isn't it just the best!

Sean Rands (10)
Stenhousemuir Primary School

A Day In The Life Of Anne Frank

Dear Kitty,
Yesterday my world was completely turned upside down. My sister got a note from a labour camp. My family were so depressed. They didn't know what to do. Finally my dad decided to go into hiding in his work attic. It was Hell and to make it worse, it wasn't just four people who were living in the attic. It was eight. My father (Otto), my mother (Edith), my older sister (Margot), me (Anne), my dad's work employee (Mr Van Daan), his wife (Mrs Van Daan), their son (Peter Van Daan), and finally a friend of the family (Mr Dussel).

Today I go through more torture. I now realise the beauty of a flower and for the wind to blow in my hair. I feel like I'm in a prison, no windows, no light, no fresh air, and no nature or wildlife around me. Every noise I hear makes me think the German soldiers are coming for me, but what really bugs me about this life is having to sit like baby mice, 24 hours a day. If I ever get out of this cramped space I will never take for granted any moment of my life.

Shannon Hurst (10)
Stenhousemuir Primary School

A Day In The Life Of Adolf Hitler

My name is Adolf Hitler. I was born in Austria on April the 20th. I left school on the 14th of June at the age of 16.

In 1903 my father died. As a boy until the age of twenty or thirty I had the dream of being an artist. My dream never came true. I failed an audition for an Austrian school of art. After that I never dreamed of being an artist again.

In 1933 I became a chancellor of Germany and then I had the idea to become an overall leader of Germany. In 1938 Germany occupied Austria and I planned to make a new world war called World War II.

In 1939 Germany invaded Poland and it was the Nazi party who were the main party involved in the invasion. In 1933 I also killed 6,000,000 or more Jews. I managed to kill them by putting them in gas chambers. I particularly remember when I sent my soldiers out to kill millions of Jews in their homes and I told my soldiers to wait for them to come out of hiding and then they killed them. In 1945 I got married to Eva Brown, and in the same year we both committed suicide.

Claire Mackie (10)
Stenhousemuir Primary School

A Day In The Life Of Baden-Powell

My name is Robert Baden-Powell. I was born in the 1880s. Once I left school I joined the army. I eventually became an officer and I was in charge. I left the army and thought younger people should be allowed to develop the skills needed to join the army. I ran a test camp in 1907 with six boys and they loved it. Scouting became very popular and a few days ago I became chief scout of the world.

I was very nervous but also proud that something I had thought up had become so popular. There were thousands of young boys all there waiting to see me become chief scout of the world. I was then called on stage. I was feeling very proud and excited but also very nervous. I was having to read out a speech in front of thousands of people. When I was ready to leave the stage I said thank you, to the crowd, for making me chief scout of the world.

Christopher Smith (10)
Stenhousemuir Primary School

A DAY IN THE LIFE OF ROBERT BURNS

My name is Robert Burns. I was born on the 25th January 1759 in a two room thatched cottage in Alloway, 'bout two miles fae Ayr. I describe the cottage as the 'auld clay biggin'. I had seven brothers and sisters, I was the eldest. I was also the only one wae heart disease, all because my youth was spent working on the farm which didnae help ma health.

In 1787 I eventually married Jean Armoir, the mother of me twins. I started writing poems and then ma first book wis publishcd in Kilmarnock in 1786. It was called Poem Il Cheifly, in Scottish dialect. I wrote many poems an' songs includin' Tam O'Shanter an' To A Mouse'. Here's an extract from 'To A Mouse'.

Wee sleekit, cowrin, tim'rous beastie
O' what a panic's in thy breastie!
Thou need na start awa sae hasty,
Wi bickering brattle!
I wad be laith to rin an' chase thee
Wi murdring prattle!

This was one of my favourite poems except fae 'Ae Fond Kiss' 'cause I wrote it for Mrs Agnes McLehose after I met her for the last time in December 1791. I also wrote two masterpieces, Tam O'Shanter an' Auld Lang Syne. I also wrote the Selkirk Grace:
Some hae meat and canna eat,
And some wad eat that want it,
But we hae meat and we can eat
Sae let the Lord be thankit.

Then I didnae ken that ma poems wid be heard every year bi school children and that people wid hae a day dedicated to me.

Stacey Skelton (10)
Stenhousemuir Primary School

A Day Of Being Invisible

One day when I woke up I wondered where I was because I wasn't in my bedroom. I didn't know where I was and suddenly a butler came in and said, 'What would you like for breakfast?'
'Em, sausages and waffles,' I said. I got up and had a look around. I went into the bathroom. I looked at myself in the mirror and said, 'Why don't I see myself?' I found out that I was living in Ibiza.

Then I suddenly had an idea! I had my breakfast and then I went to school. I sneaked onto the bus and when I got off I played tricks on people. So I tapped Catlin's shoulder, she turned round and said, 'Who's there?' No one was there, well I was but she couldn't see me. So she just walked away. When I got into the classroom I played lots of tricks on people. First I started throwing things at the teacher and she blamed it on other people. Then I started to think of other plans to trick people. As someone was about to sit I pulled their chair away from them and she fell right to the ground. Everyone was laughing, including the teacher. When the bell went I went home for lunch.

I went to the chip shop and got a bag of chips. I didn't even need to pay for them because no one would see me but I decided to pay. I left some money beside the till. I was still hungry so I went to the shop and got some sweets. I went back up to the school and I was so bored outside so I played some more tricks on people. A few boys were playing football. One of them passed to another boy then he tried to score but he missed. So I got the ball and scored. It was time to go back into the school. When we got back into the classroom I couldn't be bothered to listen to the teacher. After all, I was invisible. Why should I listen to the teacher when I could be having fun?

So I went away to the funfair. I got prizes and went on rides. Then I decided to go back to the mansion. Then I had my dinner, it was pasta. After that I had ice cream. There was vanilla, strawberry and chocolate.

I was very tired after all that so I went to sleep. And when I woke up I was back home. I told everyone about my adventure but they never believed me.

Kelsey Gibb (9)
Stenhousemuir Primary School

A Day In The Life Of Elvis Presley

My name is Elvis Aaron Presley. I was born in a two-room house in Tupelo, Mississippi on January 8th 1935. My twin brother Jessie Garon Presley was stillborn, leaving me as an only child. As a child I was raised in Memphis, where I sang church music, and I listened to the black musicians perform the blues on the radio. I was drafted into the US army in 1958. I served my national service in the army in Germany. I was discharged in 1960. On my way back to America from Germany my plane stopped in the UK, at Prestwich airport. I couldn't believe my eyes as I saw how many people were waiting for me. There were lots of screaming girls too. This was the only time I visited the United Kingdom.

When I was 13 years old, I moved with my family to Memphis, Tennessee. I began recording there for the Sun Records in 1954. 1955 was the year that was to change my life. I met Colonel Tom Parker, a successful promoter of country and western singers. He soon became my manager.

In total I wrote and released 45 hit songs. Here are some of them: Heartbreak Hotel, Don't Be Cruel, Hound Dog, Love Me Tender and Blue Suede Shoes. I also starred in 33 successful films. One of them is called Love Me Tender, making me one of the most influential and respected figures in the history of rock.

Rebecca Wilson (10)
Stenhousemuir Primary School

A Day In The Life Of Alexander Graham Bell

My name is Alexander Graham Bell. I was born on March the 3rd 1847 in Edinburgh. The one thing people remember me for is inventing the telephone. I spent one year at private school, two years at Edinburgh's Royal High School and then I graduated at the age of 14. I then attended a few lectures at Edinburgh University.

I had a thought in my mind that I could invent something so spectacular that could shock the world. I hoped to invent a device that you could contact someone far or near by tapping a button.

I believed that people couldn't contact each other and they had to go in car, by foot or other transport. I then moved to Boston to try to achieve my goal. What I had in my mind was a speaker, a bit like a trombone, a set of ear phones and a wooden box with lots of complicated wires and mechanical pieces.

After lots of unlucky tries I finally made a perfect piece of work. It turned out just the way I had imagined it to be. I called my device the telephone. I was very proud of my invention.

John McAleer (10)
Stenhousemuir Primary School

A Day In The Life Of Neil Armstrong

My name is Neil Armstrong. I was born on a farm in Wapakanveta in the state of Ohio in 1930. I worked for the state of Ohio as an auditor and I travelled throughout the state checking the finances of towns and cities of Ohio.

I was eleven years old when my family moved to Upper Sandusky in Ohio. My best interest was building model planes of different materials. Me and my friends would fly them, together sometimes from the upstairs window in my house. When I grew to the age of fourteen, I started work at the airport and washed planes to earn pocket money so that I could learn more about aircraft design.

I went to a different school to learn how to become a pilot and how to fly a plane. I took my first flying lesson at the age of fifteen. Then I took a test. I passed the test. I was an astronaut.

I was the first man to walk on the moon in 1969. I felt very nervous in space. I touched the surface of the moon to see what it felt like. I came back and I was a hero. It was watched by the whole world on national television. All of that training sure paid off. Now the whole world knows that I was the first human being ever to set foot on the moon in outer space. With those famous words: 'That's one small step for man and one giant leap for mankind'.

Claire Leishman (10)
Stenhousemuir Primary School

A DAY IN THE LIFE OF A MOUSE

I woke up inside my hole because of a loud noise outside. It sounded like a hoover. The grown-ups must be cleaning up the house. I took a peak outside and I saw a mousetrap with a mouldy piece of cheese on it. Yuck! I thought. It must've been morning because the kids were running all over the place trying to get ready for school. Suddenly I heard another noise. It was my stomach rumbling because it had been ages since I last had something to eat. So, after I checked that the coast was clear, I decided to get some brekkie. But wait! The cat was still where it was last night, right outside my hole! Luckily, he was asleep. Phew. I sneaked very quietly past him into the cupboard where all the food was kept. I ran up a mop, straight onto the shelves. Yum! Look at all this food! A nibble of cheese, some crisps, and a few bites of bread later my stomach was full. What time is it? Hmm, it's sleep time again. (Hey, I'm a mouse, I have no life!) Oh no! Tom the cat has woken up. What am I going to do now? Wait, he's going to get his milk in the kitchen. Thank God for that! Now's my chance. Quickly does it. He's spotted me Almost there, almost there, made it!

Ihtishaam Ahmad (11)
Stockbridge Primary School

A Day In The Life Of My Big Sister (Her Diary)

April 13th
17.20

I can't believe how horrible Gemma was being today! I know she's having a tough time with having to move house and everything but you'd think she would want to keep the few friends she has. Oh no, I forgot she doesn't have any since we fell out. No, I shouldn't say that, I mean she's nice enough (when she's in a good mood) which is very rare nowadays. I've got to go now 'cos I'm bursting for the loo!

April 13th
18.10

I hate April the 13th. A, it's the beginning of the football tournament and B, I always have to go and stay at my gran's for a few days, and even the naughtiest person shouldn't have to go through that much torment. I'm being serious, you would simply bore yourself to death at her house and a slow and painful death it would be as well. Anyway the football tournament is the worst. Everyone has to join in. Even the ones who can't kick a ball let alone play a whole game. It's horrid because we all get mangy and muddy which I don't particularly love, though some of the more stupid ones who love getting mucky relish the thought. My mum has just called me to do the dishes so I've got to go now to have another argument! I mean I've got millions of things that are much more fun to waste my time on than washing up, but mothers will be mothers.

April 13th
18.20

Wahay! I got out of doing them by threatening my little bro that I would tell everyone that he fancies Emma Johnston. Anyway, in exactly one hour and twenty-five seconds I will have to go to my doom, Gran's house, so I'm just going to go and start packing.

April 13th
18.40

Well that's me finished packing, I'll just go to see if Brian has finished too. He has. I'll tell you what I've packed. An assorted range of different CDs, loads of chocolate in case I get a bit too depressed, some clothes, rubbish books belonging to Brian since he doesn't have enough room in his own suitcase, and my own books. Oh no, it's time to leave! My dad is calling so I'd better go. I've just got to pack you now, diary, and I promise I will write in you as soon as I get there if I'm still alive that is!
Bye!

Jennifer Rankin (12)
Stockbridge Primary School

A Day In The Life Of A Victorian Servant

My name is Anna and I'm eleven. I look after three children.

My day starts early. I dress the children, then serve them their breakfast and feed Freddie, the baby.

When it's time to go out, the children put on their coats and boots and take their hoops for a walk in the park. I bring bread to feed the ducks at the pond.

I turn around and notice Frank isn't there. How would I tell my cold, strict mistress I'd lost her child? Then I hear a rustle behind a blackberry bush. Frank is crouching there eating blackberries.

'Please don't tell Mother!' he pleaded. 'She'll lock me in a cupboard.'
'I won't breathe a word!' I said. 'Let's get a toffee apple with the money Cook gave me, but don't tell your mother.'

We walk to Mr Watt's sweetie shop and buy three toffee apples.

When we get home we have lunch and have a quiet afternoon playing cards. The children finish their jigsaw puzzle. For supper we have boiled eggs and spinach.

By six o'clock the children were tucked up in bed. After tidying up the nursery, I went downstairs to the kitchen and talked about the mistress to Edith the housemaid and Mrs Angel, the cook. Edith giggled at what I said but Mrs Angel was shocked. She said I was ungrateful and selfish. She was in a bad mood anyway.

I found an old doll to mend and all the sewing took hours. I got to sleep about eleven o'clock.

Julia Caird (10)
Stockbridge Primary School

A Day In The Life Of An Evacuee

Maggie and Tom climbed on board the train heading for Yorkshire. They walked towards the back and sat down at an empty table.

Maggie looked around the train. The table behind them was full of injured soldiers. The soldier by the window looked familiar, other than he only had one eye. She soon fell asleep.

When she woke up Tom was gone. She thought he was in the loo. After a while Tom still hadn't returned from the loo. Maggie started to look for him. In the distance she could hear his high pitched laugh. She followed the sound to the baggage cart and put her ear to the door. She could hear a man singing.
'We'll win, we'll fight, in day or night'
Maggie knew it was a soldier because he was wearing a uniform. The snack trolley was coming her way so she walked in casually.
'This is my sister Maggie,' Tom said coldly.
The soldier turned round, he only had one eye.
'Hallo, I'm General Parker, but you can call me Jock,' he said.
'Hello, I was just looking for Tom,' said Maggie.
'Okay, we'll arrive in Yorkshire soon anyway, bye.'

When they got off the train they walked to a church to get selected. An old couple called Mr and Mrs Jones picked them.

When they got to the Jones' house they found it was a chicken farm.
'It's 8.30, get your night clothes and go to bed. We'll talk in the morning,' said Mrs Jones nicely.
'Okay, night,' said Maggie.

Kate Schofield (10)
Stockbridge Primary School

A Day In The Life Of A Gargoyle

As the sun rose over the river Seine, I stared over Paris from my seat on Notre Dame. The cool breeze tickled my wrinkled face as birds appeared and foxes fled to their dens. Shop blinds opened and baguettes and croissants were on sale once more. The smell of freshly baked pastry rose up on the breeze. I took a deep breath. Heads popped out of windows, and doors swung open as people strolled onto the cobbled pavements, and set off for work, suitcases in hand. Children piled out of their houses and played tig on the way to school.

Pleasure boats sailed down the river Seine and vehicles zoomed down busy roads. A toddler wailed for sweets. A pick pocket had stolen a lady's purse, which caused a right riot. Oh, how I wished I could be down there too!

After about ten o'clock the noise of the traffic died down. I watched the daily life below, people in the park, artists drawing the river, tourists crowding round the Eiffel Tower. The same as any other day.

'Why am I so lonely?' I asked myself. I felt a big tear roll down my cheek.

Joggers were jogging, dogs were barking, and policemen were looking for the person who had robbed the old lady. If only they would ask me. I could tell them who it was!

People gathered round about me all afternoon, gawping. I gazed after them with a green eye. They could stroll around and laugh in the warmth of the evening sun while I watched from afar.

Night fell over Paris. The foxes crept out as my dreams crept over me.

Oriana Franceschi (11)
Stockbridge Primary School

One Day In The Life Of A Cat Named Spikey

Suddenly I awoke from a sleep, deeper than the sea and I found myself in my soft, bouncy basket. I heard my owner do something so I opened my eyes.
'It's okay pussywoosums, I'm only boiling the kettle,' said Mrs Jonston kindly.
Who does she think I am? Some kind of baby? Even though I am 1 I can look after myself now.

I decided that I was going to have a nice breakfast and then go outside where the flowers were blooming beautifully with colours of crimson, bright yellow and sky-blue. I walked out onto the window sill and decided to sunbathe. Suddenly I was snapped out of my daze by a buzzing noise. A bumblebee flew past and like any normal cat I ran after it!

Not knowing it I climbed onto the roof! 'Oh no,' I said to myself as I miaowed for help. No one came after a few hours so in the end I persuaded myself that they would come in the morning, so eventually I settled down to sleep. I woke up freezing and heard something.
'Spikey!'
It's Mrs Jonston! 'Miaow!' I screamed.
'Spikey!'

I've got to get to her somehow, I thought. That's it I'll climb down the chimney! So I did. I stepped into the chimney and tumbled down, collecting soot on my way and suddenly, thump. I landed as a black ball at my owner's feet.

I never chased bees again!

Aimée Hooper (10)
Stockbridge Primary School

A Day In The Life Of A Cat

A day in the life of a cat can either be very boring and quiet, or rather exciting and dangerous depending on whether the cat is indoors or outdoors.

It was morning and Elvis the cat had risen from a deep sleep. He stretched his long sleek legs and opened his round eyes. He looked around and noticed he was in the sitting room. With great speed he bounded off the couch, across the floor and through his owner's bedroom door. He slowly crept onto the bed and then started to miaow. With a moan the owner turned around and started to rub her eyes. She started to clap her cat. 'It's breakfast time.'

She slowly got out of bed and picked up Elvis. He jumped from her when they got to the kitchen, and he started to purr happily around her legs. Two minutes later his mouth was buried in a big bowl of cat food that Elvis thought was very tasty. He then went to the litter box. With great relief he headed towards the back door and purred once more to get out.
'Okay Elvis, you can go out, I'll get more sleep that way.' She opened the door and he jumped outside.

Suddenly a bird dived from the sky just missing Elvis' eye. He lashed out at the bird just missing it. After a few moments he calmed down, and thought to himself, I'll get that bird later! He marched off with his tail swishing. Before he had gone very far he was ambushed! Four cats attacked him! He recognised two of them, they were the Fishy gang who ruled the alleyways of Leith and they meant business.

The leader was called Smokey, with dark grey hair, and he was quite chubby. The second he knew was called Jailbird, and he was very thin like Elvis but he was brown and black whereas Elvis was just black. The other two smaller cats Elvis had not seen before.

'When was I seeing you last?' spat Smokey.
The small cats giggled at this, though it was not very funny.
'I . . . I . . . I don't know,' stammered Elvis as he backed up.
'So come to the alley then, it'll be like old times before ya got an owner.'
'No thanks,' Elvis whispered.
'Ha,' Smokey laughed. 'Jailbird, get those twins, I think they sneaked off.'
'Yeah,' said Smokey to Elvis, 'the twins will teach you better to mess with the Fishys.'

A moment later Jailbird and the twins arrived with heavy smirks.
'Elvis, meet my twins, Borris and Morris.'
They looked nothing like their father Smokey. They were Persians and very fat and looked as though they had run head-first into a brick wall, with flat faces and white fur sticking out everywhere.
'Belch! We want food and now,' they screamed.
'Okay, okay, you can have food as long as you beat him up first!' snarled Smokey.

Suddenly there was a 'Woof' and then silence. Everyone paused, and then a gigantic German Shepherd ran straight into the Fishy gang and sent them rolling away. Elvis didn't look again. He just kept running and running until he got home! He ran through the cat flap and into his owner's arms.

'Where have you been?' cooed his owner.
Elvis just miaowed. But that miaow sounded like trouble.

Sam Scott-Moncrieff (10)
Stockbridge Primary School

A Day In The Life Of A Model

I woke up at 5.00am, put on my clothes and started to brush my hair. It was all hard from the hair gel that I had on the day before.

At 6.30am I left my flat and started to head towards the modelling agency in a cab.

I met my boss, Mr Tony Guy. He said that I had four fashion shows and one catwalk. They were both in Milan so I had to leave straight away.

We finally arrived in Milan. My boss took me to the modelling studio where I got my make-up done by a really nice Spanish lady. She did not speak much English so it was very quiet at points. She put pink eye shadow on me and a really horrible red lipstick. I didn't like it but it wasn't up to me. For the first fashion show I was to be a lady in pink and red. I wore a pink skirt which was very weird. I also wore a pale, pink top. It was very uncomfortable.

Finally I got out from under the boiling fashion show lights. Then I was rushed back to the make-up lady where I had to go through the whole process three more times. It was very boring.

When I did the cat walk it went a lot more smoothly than the fashion shows.

Finally I had finished. It was 9.00pm and all I wanted to do was sleep.

Sabine Whittle (11)
Stockbridge Primary School

A Day In The Life Of A Kitten

I'm going to tell you a story about a kitten called Samson who is 10 months old. Samson, who was adventurous and wild, was always getting in trouble. Okay, down to the story.

One day a kitten called Samson was chasing a mouse round the house. The mouse went under a couch which was knocked over by a rampaging Samson. The mouse went outside and Samson went after it.

Soon Samson had caught it and tried to take his dinner back to his house but he couldn't find it. Samson went around the street for ages but still couldn't find his house.

Two hours had passed since Samson had been home and he was getting hungry. He missed his basket and his mum, he wanted to go home.

Soon Samson found some dead mice to eat. Once Samson had eaten the mice he tried to get some sleep but couldn't because of the traffic. Then someone found Samson and took Samson to the pound.

When Samson was at the pound, a dog called Smasher said, 'Hey Kitti,'
'What is it?' said Samson. 'What do you want?'
'I want you to get out of my *territory!*'
'No, it's not your territory.' Then Samson dug a hole out of the pound and saw his home past a farm and a river.

It was sunset when Samson got home. He told his mum what happened, had some dinner and went to bed.

James Cummings (10)
Stockbridge Primary School

A Day In The Life Of . . . A Crisp Packet

On Monday, at five minutes to nine or another way of putting it is when the corner shop opens, also that is the time that the school bell rings, a boy aged about ten rushed into the dark, musty shop and grabbed a packet of cheese and onion crisps. After he had paid for them he ran out of the shop and along to the school where he stuffed them in his tray till break time. The tray was cracked and the corner of the crisp packet got stuck. It was not a very comfortable position to be in at all. The packet only had to turn and half the packet would be covered in old, mouldy banana!

As break finally arrived and the boy opened the packet, he ate the crisps and threw the foil packet on the ground. It floated along the ground and through the gates where it twisted up and up and up. Nobody saw, nobody bothered. It was just another piece of litter.

The packet flew up and down into a river to race with many other crisp packets. It wound in and out of twigs, sweet wrappers and other pieces of litter, till a child fished it out of the river with a net. Before she could see what it was it flew out of the net and drifted in the air until it fell from the sky like a fallen foil, cheese and onion angel, only to be squashed by cars.

Kathleen Renwick (10)
Stockbridge Primary School

THE BAT

Silence, silence, in the night,
Swooping stealthily, drinking deeply
From the cows, it likes to bite
Creeping, slinking, always thinking.

Is the nocturnal demon.

Suddenly it hears
(It has amazing ears)
The inaudible patter of tiny feet
And swoops down, without thinking
And almost instantly, he is drinking!

Iain Glen (11)
Mary Erskine & Stewart's Melville Junior School

A Close Encounter

The vicious river pike,
Makes not a sound,
As it slices through the water, dinner bound.
Out of a crevice, a trout poked its head.
Little did it know that it would soon be dead.

The pike felt a vibration in the serene waters,
Its dorsal fin went erect.
It wheeled about in a frenzy,
As it tried to detect the smell of the trout.

Ben Ellis (11)
Mary Erskine & Stewart's Melville Junior School

THE EAGLE

Up high, amongst the leaves the eagle stands proud,
Keeping himself from screeching aloud,
Standing there, he is always peering,
For a little creature sleeping or creeping,
In the dense grassland surrounding.

He sees his prey while planning his move,
In his head he thinks that he should prove
Who is boss around here and that he is dangerously near.
So he fluffs up his chest and with no fear,
Jumps off the branch and into flight,
And on his face a look of delight.

He keeps an eye while he is soaring,
On the creature who is snoring.
Sometimes sleeping,
But still keeping,
His eye on the mass,
In the withering grass.

Soon he makes a dip,
Further down to get a grip
Of his little helpless prey,
Sleeping soundly in the hay.
Very closely he approaches,
And slows down as he poaches,
The little creature who lurches.

In a glint, the eagle grabs,
And with his talons, strongly stabs
His little timorous tense prey,
And takes it to a pile of hay,
Where he tears bit by bit for the chicks in his nest,
While convincing himself he's still the best.

Matthew Henderson (11)
Mary Erskine & Stewart's Melville Junior School

A Day In The Life Of . . .

A day in the life of Kym from Hear'say.

Hi! I'm Kym from Hear'say!

9am
Today we are performing at the Brit Awards. I am so excited. First thing in the morning we check the newspaper. We check the newspaper because the press make up stories and lies about us!

9.30am
I have a shower and get ready for a rehearsal! Now I go and wake Suzanne up. I go downstairs and have a cup of tea and some toast. I telephone my mother to tell her how I am and to speak to my two children, Emily and David.

11am
I have just got back from rehearsing. We shall go back to the studio in two hours. Now I have lunch with Myleene, Suzanne, Noel and Danny.

1pm
We go back to the studio now and get ready and have another rehearsal. Now it is 4.30. We have dinner.

6pm
Now I am really nervous and excited, we are on in about an hour. Now we go for a look around the studio. We meet Destiny's Child, Robbie Williams and Westlife.

6.40pm
We have twenty minutes to get prepared for our performance. We are on after Destiny's Child.

We have just finished performing. I think it went well. Except for some boos from the press.

One hour later; the Brits are just about to finish. We are about to go to a celebration party.

We have just got home. I have a drink and go to bed. This was one of the best days of my life.

Victoria Gillies (11)
Wilton Primary School

A Day In The Life Of Minnie

I wake up by the sound of doors slamming and people shouting. I can't seem to get out of bed though. It's so warm and comfy. 'I wonder what I'll have for breakfast?' I say to myself.

'Hi Minnie!' says my owner.
'Leave me alone!' I moan while I pull my blanket over my belly. Suddenly my mum comes in and I run to meet her. I'm always happy to see her in the morning because she's the one who gives me my breakfast. She walks to the fridge and pulls out an orange plastic box.
'My breakfast, my breakfast!' I say excitedly.
She takes off the lid and that lovely smell of chicken fills the kitchen. I watch it in the microwave, just sitting there! When it's ready it is put outside for me to eat because it smells so bad when it's hot! I gulp it down so nobody else can eat it.

After breakfast is when the fun begins. I can now do my favourite thing in the world, guard the rabbits! But first I have to get comfy. Once I'm comfy I can basically guard the rabbits. It's heaven.

It's now time for my walk. I love walks so much. When I get down the drive there are always cats waiting. But I am on a lead so I can't chase them. What a shame! During my walk I see lots of things and smell lots of different smells. When I get up to the woods I'm let off the lead. I run and run, under roots, over tree stumps, that's the life!

All of that running makes me tired, so I cuddle down into my nice, warm, comfy basket and fall asleep.

Mairi Cameron (10)
Wilton Primary School

A Day In The Life Of A Tiger!

One day on the 29th of September I woke up after a bad dream. I was bathing beside a little shallow river, the sun was beating down on me. I let out a yawn. It was strange because instead of a normal yawn I let out a roar. I walked round and I looked in the river. I saw my reflection but it was a tiger! I was astonished.

I was looking at the other side of the river. There was a hare drinking at the side of the river. I was rather hungry so I plucked up my courage and ran across the river. The hare saw me and ran full pelt into the bushes. Eventually I caught it and ate it.

I heard someone talking to me, it came out of a bush surrounded by giant sycamore trees. It said, 'Hello, my name is Fraya but everybody calls me Frai! What's yours?'
'Emily but my nickname is Emi. Where do you live?' I said.
'I live at Jungle Hollow, would you like to come to our den?'
'Okay.'
We got to Jungle Hollow and Frai introduced me to her family, then we went hunting for tea. I got a rat for mine. Me and Frai went jumping trees. We followed a squirrel, but it ran into its drey. At last we got to Frai's favourite tree. It was that comfy I fell asleep.

Emily Rafferty (10)
Wilton Primary School

A DAY IN THE LIFE OF MY KITTEN

If I was my kitten I would sleep half the day. I'd play outside in the rain and splosh in the puddles and get soaking wet. I'd play with my friends and chase all the birds and all the flies. I'd go through all the gaps that I couldn't fit through when I was big. I'd love to be a cat, I'd crawl through all those gaps. I would scare the mice and all the spiders. I'd wag my tail and puff it up to warn my predators. I'd also chase my tail. I'd also pounce on the other cats.

At night I would wander to and fro to places I've never been before in my whole entire life. I'd fall asleep and dream a happy dream. I'd dream I was a flying cat, also an aqua cat but I know cats could never really fly or swim in their life, but the Egyptians did think so. I'd also creep through the dark. My eyes would glisten in the moonlight. I'd be starving through the night because my owners would be asleep. I'd also chase the piles of grass that roll about in the night. I'd miaow in the middle of the night and hopefully my owners would come down and feed me. Then I'd be tucked up in bed. But when they would go away I would get out of bed and go out to play with my midnight friends.

Shaun Cooper (10)
Wilton Primary School

A Day In The Life Of A Puppy

One day I woke up and found myself lying in a dog basket. I jumped up suddenly feeling confused and I looked around. I was in the Battersea Dog's Home. Why was I here? Then I found that I had fur on my back. That was when I realised that I was a puppy! A few seconds later a lady came in with a ball for me to play with and a bowl full of dog food. The dog food looked nice and tasty but I didn't know whether to take it or not in case it made me sick. Then I finally decided to taste it, so I went over to the bowl and took a mouthful. It was delicious so I decided to eat it all.

Afterwards I was full and couldn't be bothered to play with my ball, so I lay in my bed and began to look out the window watching for somebody to come along and take me home with them, but nobody came. Nobody even bothered to look at me. They were all looking at the collie dog next door or the black Labrador across from me. I began to feel sad and put my head and ears down low.

Then I sat up quickly and looked out the window and there, to my surprise, was a little girl of about four, staring at me through the glass. I stared back at her. Then she pointed at me and spoke to a lady. They disappeared a few seconds later, so I decided to go back to my basket.

Then the door opened and a lady came in and picked me up. I noticed the little girl again and barked. She smiled and followed me. The next thing I knew I was getting put into a small cage and then into the boot of a car. The car started moving and I barked as I got a fright.

When the car stopped I heard a few bangs and then someone opened the boot and took me out and carried me into a house. Then I saw the little girl again and barked. She came over, patted me on the back and said, 'Tod!' I guessed that must have been my name.

That night I slept in a comfy bed. In the morning when I woke up I was back to normal, in my own bed and quite glad to be too.

Sian Henderson (11)
Wilton Primary School

A Day In The Life Of . . .

A day in the life of Suzanne from Hear'say.

'Hi, I'm Suzanne.'

9.00am
Today we are going to the Pepsi Chart Show. That doesn't start until 7.00pm but we will be going at round about 5.30pm for rehearsals. First thing's first, we better get ready because we are allowed to visit our families. I'm going to visit my mum, dad and the rest of my family. Kym is visiting Emily, her daughter, and David, her son, who live with her mum and dad. Noel is visiting his mum and all his aunties and uncles. Danny is visiting his mum and all his aunties and uncles as well.

9.30am
We are going to get ready for another day. Myleene is going for a shower. I'm getting my make-up on then I will do my hair. Danny and Noel are already away to visit their families.

11.15am
Paul Adams is taking me, Kym and Myleene to visit our families. We arrived there at round about 11.15am. Me and Myleene went to Kym's house. Then we went to my house, then at last we went to Myleene's house.

3.30pm
At 3.30pm we are going for rehearsals to practice for Pure And Simple, because that is what we are singing at the Pepsi Chart Show.

5.00pm
At 5.00pm everybody was getting ready. At 5.15pm we were all ready. At 5.30 we arrived at the Pepsi Chart Show. We were first on, singing Pure And Simple.

9.30pm
At 9.30pm we got in. Me, Kym and Myleene all went to bed because we were really tired.

11.00pm
Danny and Noel went to bed at 11.00pm.

That is the end of another day.

Rachel Gibson (10)
Wilton Primary School

A Day In The Life Of A Rabbit

One day I was in the pet shop. I was nibbling away on some carrot when kids came in. I started to drink and suddenly they walked towards me. I walked back. They called the shopkeeper and she took me out of my hutch and gave me to them.

The shopkeeper put me in a cardboard box. I did not like it as it was dark and it scared me. We stopped. The box was put on the floor. When it was opened a child of about five was standing looking at me. I was her birthday present. I was taken out of the box and placed in her arms. I jumped straight back out of them and ran into the garden, as the door was open. I dug a hole through to the next garden.

Suddenly two kids ran out and picked me up and put me in a hutch. There was a knock at the door and I heard people talking, then the people who had bought me came and took me back to their garden.

The little girl came to lift me out and I made a bid for freedom and hopped until I was back at the pet shop. Libby, the pet shop owner, picked me up and put me in one of her hutches. I had a sore leg so Libby took me to the vet and it was discovered that I had a broken leg.

I was taken back to my owners. I jumped again and hobbled towards the road. A car came and I was run over. Everything was blurry and I felt strange and I started twitching.

I woke up and I was taken home, but I wasn't going to give up and I hobbled towards a field. I found some babies and decided they would be mine. A fox came, so did my owners and just in time. They took us all home.

They said I must want to be a mum and gave me the babies to look after. They called me Holly and my kids, Bill, Billy, Angela, Angie, Bex and Rebecca.

Rebecca Richardson (11)
Wilton Primary School

A Day In The Life Of My Mum

Today I have a study day which means that I don't have to get up at 6.00 in the morning to go to Napier University for lectures. Instead I can lie in until 7.30 to see to the children before they go to school.

I get up at 7.30 and have a cup of coffee before I wake up my two children. I wake them up at 7.45 and tell them to have a shower while I make their breakfast. I collect all the dirty washing and put it into the washing machine while the children eat their breakfast. I prepare their packed lunches before making sure that they have all their books for the day at school. My children set off to school at 8.30 and I continue my daily tasks. I wash and dry the breakfast dishes and the night before's supper dishes.

By now it is about 9.00 and I go for a shower. After my shower I hang the washing out then make the beds. My duties for the next hour or so include washing the kitchen floor, hoovering the living room, dinette and stairs, polishing the furniture in the living room before I finally sit down for another cup of coffee. I do some studying until about 1.00 then I have my lunch.

The next thing I do is bring the washing in and iron for about an hour. I then do some more studying until the children come in from school. The children get changed to do their homework and have a snack while I prepare the dinner. After dinner my husband helps me to wash and dry the dishes. My son goes out to football training and my daughter goes out to play with her friends.

I now have some time to spend with my husband before the children come home. I prepare supper about 8.30 while the children have a shower. They then have their supper before they go to bed at about 9.00. I tidy up and have some supper before my husband and myself go to bed.

Lynsi Waldie (10)
Wilton Primary School